The First Time Ever Published.

The Fourth Classic Diner Mystery

From *New York Times* Bestselling Author

Jessica Beck

A BAKED HAM

Other Books by Jessica Beck

The Donut Shop Mysteries

Glazed Murder
Fatally Frosted
Sinister Sprinkles
Evil Éclairs
Tragic Toppings
Killer Crullers
Drop Dead Chocolate
Powdered Peril
Illegally Iced

The Classic Diner Mysteries

A Chili Death
A Deadly Beef
A Killer Cake
A Baked Ham

The Ghost Cat Cozy Mysteries

Ghost Cat: Midnight Paws

Jessica Beck is the *New York Times* Bestselling Author of the Donut Shop Mysteries from St. Martin's Press and Author of The Classic Diner Mystery Series and The Ghost Cat Cozy Mysteries from Cozy Publishing.

To every man and woman working the grill!

A BAKED HAM: Copyright © 2013

All rights reserved.

Chapter 1

Given what I knew about the murder victim, it was probably a shame that no one but the killer saw Benjamin Barrymore Booth's final performance. Knowing Benny, I doubt that he had died conventionally without his fair share of drama; after all, it just wasn't his style. I thought it odd when Benny failed to take the stage during Jasper Fork Community Theater's opening night of their production of *The Last Man Left*, but when the sheriff came out to announce what had happened to the actor, nobody was more surprised than me.

Ordinarily, the whole thing wouldn't have had that much of an impact on my everyday life, but there was a complication, as there always seemed to be around my family and me. The problem was that *both* of my grandparents had just taken part in a rather public argument with the dead man less than an hour before he'd shuffled off this mortal coil, and that put me, my family, and my staff from The Charming Moose Diner right in the middle of another murder investigation.

It might help if I backed up a little.

My name's Victoria Nelson, and along with my somewhat eccentric extended family, I run The Charming Moose Diner, a quaint little place located in Jasper Fork, North Carolina.

Twenty minutes before the play in question was set to begin, I was standing in the lobby of the community theater when I squeezed my husband's hand. "I'm so excited that we're going to see a real play." We were both outfitted nicely for the occasion, me in a black dress that managed to make me look trim despite the fact that I was nothing of the sort, and Greg wearing the only suit he owned. There was no doubt that my husband looked dashing, but it was a little startling seeing the handsome man I'd married in anything but blue jeans, a T-shirt, and an apron. Greg's work behind the grill at our diner would ruin that suit in thirty seconds, but sometimes I forgot just how dashing my husband looked when he was all cleaned up.

"I don't know how *real* it's going to be," Greg said with a grin. "With Benny Booth playing the lead, I'm not expecting too much."

"He does tend to get a little carried away with his roles at times, doesn't he?" I asked.

"Are you kidding me? He's the biggest ham this side of Hormel," Greg said. "It's going to take every ounce of my restraint not to bust out laughing when he starts emoting like he does."

I squeezed his hand a little harder for just a second. "You'll manage to contain yourself, though, right?"

"Victoria, I'll be so good you'll think I fell asleep, which just might happen if this play is going to be as bad as folks are saying it will."

"That I don't mind one bit. As long as you don't snore, you'll be fine," I said. I was about to add something else when I heard a familiar voice shouting on the other side of the theater lobby.

"Benny, are you on drugs, or have you just lost your mind? I can't believe that you made a pass at my wife right in front of me! Keep your hands to yourself, or I swear right here and now that I'll break them both off and feed them to you if you ever try something like that again!"

That was my grandfather's voice, there was no mistaking it, and he was angry.

"Come on. Let's go," I told my husband as I started pulling him through the crowd toward the argument.

"Finally, things are starting to get interesting," Greg said with a slight smile as he allowed himself to be led. He was long used to my grandfather; in fact, the two of them were as close as they could be. I wasn't quite so amused by the spectacle myself. The last thing I wanted was for Moose to get into any serious trouble.

"I assure you," Benny said, "that I never touched your wife."

"You just patted my fanny, and you know it!" Martha said. Normally my grandmother was a calm and levelheaded woman, but at that moment, she was as angry as I'd ever seen her in my life.

"That's it," Moose said as he started to take his suit jacket off. "Now you're insulting us both by trying to lie about what you did. You're going to pay for that, Bennie boy, and I'm the man who's going to collect the bill."

I was about to try to stop things from escalating further when Sheriff Croft stepped in between the two men. The sheriff looked grim as he clamped one hand down on Moose's shoulder, and the other on Benny's. Not many men in Jasper Fork could restrain my grandfather with one hand, and even less would be willing to try it, despite my grandfather's age, but the sheriff didn't even blink.

As expected, Moose didn't take particularly kindly to the lawman's touch. "Let me go," my grandfather said as he fought to pull away from the sheriff. "I have a score to settle with this over-baked ham, and I mean to do it right here and now."

Greg stepped in at that moment and put his own hand on Moose's other shoulder. "Take it easy, my friend," he said in an easy voice. "We both know that this isn't the time or the place."

"What if he'd tried something like that with your wife?" Moose asked my husband angrily.

"If he'd grabbed *my* behind, he'd have pulled back a stub," I said. "Greg's right, though. Settle down, Moose."

"Victoria, this isn't any concern of yours. I'm handling the situation just fine all by myself," my grandfather replied.

"Funny, it looked as though you could use some help from where I was standing." I noticed that the crowd around us was deadly silent, paying careful attention to every word uttered in our argument, no doubt so that they could repeat it all faithfully back later, with their own embellishments added, of course. I couldn't really blame them. They were probably getting a better show in the lobby than they'd ever see on stage.

"You're needed backstage, Mr. Booth," a young man with a clipboard said urgently.

"Sorry, but I must go," Benny said with great flourish. He turned to the sheriff and asked, "Will you kindly release me, Officer? I am needed, and after all, the show must go on."

The sheriff let Benny go, and the actor stepped quickly away while my grandfather was still being restrained by both Greg and the sheriff.

As Benny made his way through the crowd, Moose yelled out, "This isn't finished, you over-baked ham, not by a long shot."

Once the actor was safely out of sight, Moose looked at the sheriff and Greg as he calmly said, "There's no need to restrain me now. You can both let me go."

"Only if you promise me that you're not going to do anything about Benny Booth," Sheriff Croft said.

My grandfather bit his lower lip as he shook his head. "If that's what it's going to take to release me, you might as well lock me up, Sheriff, because that's a promise I won't make."

The sheriff frowned, and then he turned to me. "Victoria, will *you* promise to watch him?"

"Thanks, but no thanks," I said with a laugh. "There is no *way* that I'm taking on that obligation." Moose looked pleased by my refusal, but clearly my grandfather misunderstood my intent. I hadn't turned the responsibility down out of loyalty to him so much as to refuse to take on that kind of overwhelming charge.

"Don't worry. I'll watch him," Greg said.

"Just as long as *somebody* does," Sheriff Croft said as he released Moose. Greg quickly followed suit, and as soon as Moose was free, he started for the nearest exit.

"Where are you going now?" the sheriff asked.

"Anywhere but here," Moose said. "If you think I'm going to go in there now, you've lost your mind." My grandfather made his way through the crowd, which parted as though it had no choice, and soon enough Moose stormed out through the front door of the theater.

"Oh, dear, I don't like the looks of that. I'd better go after him," Martha said as she headed for the door herself.

"I've got a better idea. Why don't you stay and watch the play with Victoria, and I'll go after him myself?" Greg suggested. "Don't worry about me. I can handle Moose."

"No thank you. As much as I appreciate your kind offer, Greg, I'd better be the one who goes after him. You two stay, though, and enjoy yourselves."

"I'm not so sure that *I* still want to see this performance after what just happened," I said.

"Come on, Victoria," Greg said. "You've been looking forward to this for weeks. Don't let one idiot spoil the entire experience for you."

"I agree," Martha said. "We know how much you love us both, but this is our battle, not yours. Now, I really must go catch up with your grandfather before he does something that we'll all end up regretting later."

After Martha was gone as well, I asked Greg, "Are you sure we shouldn't go after them?"

"Given the circumstances, I doubt that either one of us could do much good, and besides, Benny's as safe from your grandfather right now as he'll ever be. Moose wouldn't dare attack him while he's onstage."

"I think that you're clearly underestimating my grandfather," I said, "but I really do want to see this performance."

"Then you're going to do just that. I'll even try to stay awake, if you think that might help matters."

"Well, it couldn't hurt," I said.

But I never got the chance to see the play at all.

It turned out that Benny was dead wrong about one thing.

The show *didn't* go on after what the sheriff announced to the crowded theater ten minutes later.

Chapter 2

"Ladies and gentlemen, I'm afraid that I've got some bad news. Tonight's performance has been cancelled."

"What happened?" someone asked from the front.

"I'm getting to that, if you'll just give me a second. It appears that someone slipped into one of the dressing rooms and killed Benny Booth."

I grabbed Greg's arm as I started to get up. "We need to find Moose and Martha."

My husband stood as well just as the sheriff said loudly, "You all need to stay right where you are until I'm finished." Was he looking straight at me as he'd said it? It surely felt that way to me. "I'm sorry for the delay, but I'm going to need to get everyone's name and address before I can let anyone leave. Now, if you'll all file out toward the back of the theater in an orderly fashion, I have officers stationed there to take down your information. It's going to take a while, but bear with us; it can't be helped. All I can promise you is that we'll make it as painless for you all as we can."

"Greg, we can't wait that long," I said as I rejected the sheriff's command and headed for the nearest exit instead of the back of the theater. It wasn't going to be easy, though. Everyone else was standing as well, and it appeared that our way was solidly blocked.

I was about to pull my husband through the crowd toward the side exit despite what the sheriff had just ordered when I heard the man himself speak to us from ten feet away.

"Victoria, Greg, I need to see you both right now, if you don't mind."

"From the tone in his voice, I have a hunch that it doesn't matter if we mind or not," Greg said softly to me.

"Let's just get this over with as quickly as we can so we can find my grandparents," I said quietly to my husband.

"I'll try to do my part," he said.

"What can we do for you, Sheriff?" I asked as I turned and looked at him.

"Not here," Sheriff Croft said as he looked around. We were getting quite a bit of attention where we stood, so Greg and I followed the sheriff back up onstage. "That's better. Victoria, where are your grandparents?"

"How should I know?" I asked. "You saw us in the audience when you came out to announce what had happened. You were remarkably restrained during your announcement, by the way. What exactly happened to Benny, anyway?"

"I'm not ready to release that information yet," Sheriff Croft said tightly.

"You can't be serious. We're going to find out soon enough," I answered. "Why don't you just save us all the trouble and tell us now?"

I wasn't sure that he'd go for it, but the sheriff finally shrugged as he said, "Keep it quiet for now; can I at least ask you to do that?"

"We won't tell anyone except family," I said.

The sheriff shook his head. "That's a pretty broad exclusion, Victoria."

"Maybe so, but it's the best I can promise you, and you know it."

"Fine," the sheriff said, and I could see the exhaustion etched in his face. I wouldn't have tried my hand at his job on a bet, though Moose and I had a little luck in the past solving a crime or two ourselves. Our efforts had strictly been on a volunteer basis, and *no one* was expecting us to save the day. Sheriff Croft, on the other hand, seemed to have a steady and unrelenting wave of crime coming at him all of the time, while Moose and I had the luxury to be able to investigate only the cases that had a direct impact on our lives, our family, and our diner.

Suddenly I was starting to have a little remorse for badgering the poor man. "It's okay. You don't have to tell us if you don't want to."

Greg looked at me with his mouth agape, but before he could say anything, the sheriff said, "No, it's okay. Somebody hit Benny in the back of the head with a trophy of some sort. Whoever did it scored a perfect hit, and he died right there on the spot."

"What kind of trophy would there be in a dressing room backstage?" Greg asked.

"One of my officers told me that it looked like a Jasper Award. I'd never heard of it myself, but it turns out that it's a local award they give to the best actor of the year in Community Theater, and Benny just won the thing. Evidently he took it with him everywhere he went. Anyway, that's what killed him. Now, can you help me find your grandparents, Victoria? I really need to track them down. Do you have any guesses where the best place to look for them might be? We've checked their home, but they aren't there."

"You don't seriously believe that either one of them could have had anything to do with this, do you? Sheriff, you've known them both your whole life."

"Frankly, I hate this part of my job," he said heatedly, "but you heard them both out in the lobby. There were threats flying around the room like seagulls tailing a trash barge."

"Check the diner," Greg told the sheriff. I stared at my husband for three seconds before he reluctantly said to me, "Victoria, I agree that this is ridiculous, but the sooner the sheriff talks to Moose and Martha, the sooner they'll be off his list of suspects and he can go after the *real* killer. I'd stake my life on the fact that neither one of *them* did it."

"Thanks for the tip," the sheriff said.

I planned to have words with Greg about what he'd just done, but I wasn't finished with the sheriff yet. "How did the killer get into the dressing room without being seen by anybody? That hallway must be jammed with people so close to the curtain."

"You've clearly never seen the dressing room Benny was

assigned. It has its own entrance from the outside. Whoever killed him could have easily slipped in from the alley, hit him, and then tore out of there before anyone but Benny even knew that they were there."

"I didn't realize that," Greg said sadly, his features sinking into despair. He looked at me and added, "Victoria, I figured that there was no way either one of them could have gone backstage without a dozen people recognizing them, so I thought that they'd both be safe."

"Don't worry about it, Greg," I said. "Neither one of them did it, so you're right. The quicker they talk to the sheriff, the better off everyone will be." I pointed to the mass of people jamming up the rear of the auditorium. "Sheriff, we helped you. Can you return the favor and let us out a side door so we don't have to go through that?"

"I don't see why not," he said. "Follow me." After a few steps, he hesitated, and then the sheriff turned to look back at us. "One thing, though. I don't want either one of you calling them to warn them that I'm coming."

"We promise not to do that, but you can't keep us from tagging along with you," Greg said. "I owe them at least that after I told you where they might be."

The sheriff just shook his head, but he didn't say no, so I was going to take that as a strong yes. Once we were outside and in our car following the police cruiser to the diner, Greg asked, "Are you sure that you're not upset with me for giving the sheriff an idea where he might look for your grandparents?"

"Don't beat yourself up about it, Greg. He would have thought of it himself in another five minutes," I said as I patted his hand. "No one's going to be upset."

Greg laughed. "Have you even *met* your grandfather, Victoria?"

I smiled slightly. "Well, he won't be upset about *just* that," I said. "I figure tonight he's going to have enough mad to go around for everyone."

"True," my husband said.

We pulled into the diner's parking lot just as the sheriff got out of his cruiser. The place was supposed to be dark and closed down at that time of night, but instead, we found that the lights were all on. Inside, Martha was on a barstool, and Moose was standing on the other side of the counter, sipping a cup of coffee. They looked for all the world like a pair without a trouble between them, but I knew better. Things were about to happen pretty quickly, and I hated that we were about to interrupt the last moment of peace either one of them was going to have for awhile.

"Let me handle this," the sheriff said as we approached the door together.

"Hang on one second. I'll unlock the door for you," I said as I reached for my keys.

"There's no need to do that," Greg said. "Moose is coming."

My grandfather opened the door, and there was a quizzical expression on his face. "What's going on? Is the play over already?"

"Somebody killed Benny in his dressing room at the theater," I said, not meaning to just blurt out the news like that.

"What happened to letting me handle it?" the sheriff asked softly. It was pretty clear that he was angry about my outburst, but I couldn't just let Moose and Martha be ambushed like that without at least knowing what had happened. "You need to leave, Victoria."

"She's not going anywhere," Greg said, "and neither am I." He then turned to my grandfather and said, "Moose, I told the sheriff that you'd probably be here. I figured the sooner we got this foolishness over with, the better. I'm sorry if I let you down."

My grandfather put a friendly hand on Greg's shoulders. "Nothing to apologize for, Son. You did the right thing."

I could see the relief flood through Greg. Moose's opinion meant a great deal to him.

My grandfather pulled his hand away, and then he turned

to Sheriff. "Now, what's this about Benny, Sheriff? Surely you don't think that *I* killed the man."

"I'm just gathering information right now. Do either one of you happen to have an alibi for the past forty-five minutes?" Sheriff Croft asked.

Moose laughed, which was not the reaction I'd been expecting. "Are you accusing *Martha* now? You're kidding, right?"

"I don't know why that's so hard to believe. I'm *just* as capable of doing it as you are, Moose," my grandmother said. "Why *shouldn't* I be a suspect?"

"Is that really a list that you *want* to be on, Martha?" he asked her as though the rest of us weren't even there.

"Of course not. I just don't want to be taken for granted, that's all."

Moose just shook his head as he looked at the sheriff. "The only alibis we have are each other. I've got a hunch that's not going to be good enough for you, is it?"

"What about when you first stormed off?" the sheriff asked. "Martha, you didn't leave for at least three minutes after your husband off, and who knows how long it took you to find him."

Martha nodded. "I suppose our alibis aren't as good as I'd hoped they be. Sorry, but I can't help you. I admit that it took me fifteen minutes to find Moose back here at the diner."

"Martha," Moose snapped. "You didn't have to tell him that."

"I want him to know the truth," she said. "A lack of a solid alibi does not make either one of us guilty of murder, Moose."

"Maybe not, but it can't help your causes," I said.

The sheriff looked at me and frowned, but at least he'd dropped that bit of nonsense about Greg and me leaving. This was our diner, and it was where we belonged.

"Are you going to arrest either one of them right now?" Greg asked.

"Of course not."

"But they're both on your list of suspects, aren't they?" I asked.

"Victoria, even you'd have to admit that I'd be a fool not to at least include them," the sheriff answered.

Moose surprised me by patting the sheriff's arm. "You would indeed. Sheriff, nobody here is blaming you for doing your job, but I'm afraid this is a dead end for your investigation."

"Martha said that she was looking for you," the sheriff said. "You never told me what you were doing."

"I was driving around," Moose said. "I hate it when my temper gets the best of me, and I didn't want to be around anybody. After ten minutes, I decided that what I really needed was a cup of coffee, so I came here and made myself one."

"There's an awful lot of time that you can't account for," the sheriff said.

"That's not strictly true. I can account for every second of it," Moose said. "What I can't do is offer you any proof that I'm telling the truth. I guess we're at a stalemate, aren't we?"

"For now," the sheriff said as he headed for the door. He hesitated before he left, though, and turned back to look at my grandparents. "You two aren't going out of town anytime soon, are you?"

"To be honest with you, we had thought about going to the fishing cabin tomorrow for a few weeks," Moose said.

"Well, I can't make you, but I'd appreciate it if you'd both hang around town, at least for now," Sheriff Croft said.

"We can do that, can't we, Martha?" he asked his wife.

"You were the one with a burning desire to go fishing," my grandmother said. "If it were up to me, we'd have stayed here all along."

"There you go, Sheriff. Can I pour you a cup of coffee to go?"

"Sure, why not," Sheriff Croft said, the weight of another

murder clearly pounding down on him. Moose poured him a paper-cup full, and the sheriff put a dollar on the counter.

"Don't worry about it. It's on the house," Moose said.

"You know me. I *always* pay my way as I go."

"Suit yourself," Moose said as he folded the bill up and tucked it into his shirt pocket.

After the sheriff was gone, I looked at my grandfather and asked, "Would you mind explaining what that was all about?"

"What are you talking about, Victoria?"

"You haven't been that nice to the sheriff since you were selling raffle tickets for your lodge," I said.

"You *were* awfully nice to him," Martha said.

"What can I say? I'm trying to turn over a new leaf," Moose said. "To be frank, I've been losing my temper too much lately, and I'm trying to change."

"*You?*" I asked incredulously. "There's got to be more to it than that."

"Granddaughter, are you questioning my truthfulness?"

"Absolutely."

Moose grinned. "Okay, I can't really blame you for that. Part of it is that I didn't want to antagonize the sheriff any sooner than I had to. I figure that as soon as he finds out that we're digging into Benny's murder, he'll have reason enough to be upset with the two of us."

I felt a sinking feeling in the pit of my stomach. "So, we're going to try to solve Benny's murder ourselves. You're right about one thing. The sheriff isn't going to be too happy about that."

"You're with me, though, aren't you?" Moose asked as he studied me carefully.

"You shouldn't even have to ask. Why don't you pour us all more coffee so we can get started?"

"None for me," Martha said. "I'll never get to sleep if I start drinking caffeine this late in the day. Honestly, I'm just going to be in the way here. I think I'll go home, if you don't mind."

"I'd be happy to drive you," Greg said.

"I don't want to put you out," Martha said.

"It's no trouble, believe me. I've found that it works out better for me if I stay our of their way when they're sleuthing. All I need is my grill and my family to be happy."

I kissed Greg's cheek. "Are you sure you don't mind?"

"I'm happy to do it. Just don't stay out too late. Remember, you've got an early start tomorrow."

"Thanks," I said.

"I could always come in and work your opening shift tomorrow," Martha offered. My grandmother used to have my job until she'd retired, and she still filled in for me every now and then. Even though she'd gotten a little careless with making change over the years, it was still wonderful having her there.

"Thanks, but until we have some kind of plan, I'm not sure when I'll need you. I plan on taking you up on your offer eventually. I'm just not sure when yet."

"There's no rush. I'm here if you need me."

"I won't be long," Moose said as he kissed my grandmother soundly.

"Don't make promises you can't keep, you old fool," she said with a laugh.

After they were gone, Moose looked at me, grinned, and rubbed his hands together. "Let's get started, shall we?"

"You're enjoying this just a little too much for my taste," I said. "A man died tonight, remember? And you're one of the sheriff's chief suspects. It's not exactly a cause for celebration. I know you weren't all that fond of Benny, but it's still no reason to smile about what happened to him."

"That wasn't why I was smiling, and you know it. You're right. Benny was a rat, but he still deserved better than to get whacked with his own trophy. The reason I smiled is because I live for these puzzles of ours. Retirement isn't all that it's cracked up to be, and a little excitement every now and then is a welcome thing."

"Funny, I could do just fine without too much of it

myself. Now, should I get our Specials board out so we can make a list of who might have clobbered Benny from behind? I mean besides you and Martha."

"That's not a bad idea. Thanks for not including our names on it. I can't imagine having too much trouble making a list. Benny wasn't exactly beloved around here, was he?"

I shook my head. "Sure, he could be annoying at times, but that's not enough reason to kill a man, is it?"

"It depends on how irritating he is," Moose said, and I swear that I couldn't tell if he was kidding or not. I decided to leave that one alone as I got the whiteboard out from behind the counter. After erasing the daily specials, I headed up the list with the word Suspect, and then I added another section and titled it Motive. It was as good as anyplace else to start, but I had a hunch that Moose and I were in for a long night.

Moose took the pen from me and started to write. "The first name on the list has to be Benny's understudy in the play. Do you have any idea who that might be?"

"Surely you're not suggesting that someone killed him just so they could play a role in a community theater production."

"People have killed for less, Victoria. Let's at least put the man's name on the board. All of this is just a starting point, remember?"

I shrugged as I pulled a playbill from my purse and scanned the names. "It says here that Fred Hitchings is playing the bartender, third man in crowd, and he's also acting as Benny's understudy. That's a lot to ask from one man, isn't it?"

"I doubt the other roles are all that large, since they don't even merit their own names," Moose said. "Fred's been a frustrated actor for years. He sells cars to earn a living, but countless times he's told me that he nearly went to Hollywood when he was younger. It had to be to take a tour, because he's *never* been any good as an actor. As bad as

Benny was, at least the man could remember his lines."
Moose wrote Jealousy beside Fred's name, and then asked,
"Who's next?"

"How about Vern Jeffries?" I suggested. "He and Benny
were on the outs over their insurance business, weren't they?
From what I heard here at the diner last month, Vern nearly
choked the life out of Benny right there in their office."

"That sounds like reason enough to me," Moose said as
he wrote Vern's name down.

"Were there any women in Benny's life?" I asked.

"I doubt that any sane lady in town would go out with the
guy," Moose said.

"Don't sell Benny short," I said. "Whether you liked the
man or not, he could be quite charming when he wanted to
be. It wouldn't surprise me a bit if he had something going
with his costar."

Moose looked surprised by the suggestion. "I suppose
it's worth a shot. Who's his current leading lady?"

I didn't have to get the playbill out this time. "It's Sandra
Hall. The reason I know that is because she was in the diner
three days ago with a brooding young man. He was pretty
solicitous towards her, and to be honest with you, she seemed
a little uncomfortable with the intensity of his attention. I'm
sorry, but I have no idea what the man's name was."

"Give me a second and I'll find out," Moose said. "I
need to make a few telephone calls. Maybe I can find out."
My grandfather moved to a far booth as he pulled out his cell
phone.

While he was gone, I took the time to wipe down the
counter again. It didn't really need it, but it was something to
do, a nervous tic of mine that helped pass the time.

"I got it," Moose said with a grin as he grabbed the pen
and wrote down the name Marcus Jackson. After it, he wrote
Jealousy again. "He's a personal trainer at the same gym
where Sandra works."

"I fully realize that the meanings are different, but you
used the same word to describe two completely different

situations."

"I can fix that," Moose said as he added the word Romantic next to Marcus's name. "Is that better?"

"Much. Who else do we have?"

We both thought about it, and then Moose said, "I have a hunch this list isn't going to be our final one. I'm pretty sure we'll add a few more names as we keep digging."

"And hopefully strike a few out along the way as well," I said. "I think we're both tapped out for tonight. What do you think?"

"Let me record our list on a sheet of paper, and then we can go," Moose said as he got out an order pad and started jotting the names down.

I took out my cell phone and snapped a quick picture of the board.

"What did you just do?" Moose asked me.

"You take your notes your way, and I'll do mine my way," I said. "Tell me when you're finished and I'll erase the board."

"Let's just stow it away in back until we need it again," Moose said. "You're not planning on running any new specials this week, are you?"

"With Greg, I never know. If he gets an itch to make something new, I've given him my blessing to do it."

"Well, until you need it, let's keep recording our thoughts here." Moose picked up the board and walked into the kitchen with it.

I called out, "I'm dumping the coffee pot. Do you want the last bit?"

"No, thanks. I probably shouldn't drink what I have left in my cup. It's going to be a long night, all in all."

"Because of the caffeine?" I asked.

"That's the least of it. I know that I may have sounded cavalier when I talked to the sheriff about Benny's murder, but there's a lot about it that bothers me."

"Could it be based on the fact that you and Martha are the sheriff's key suspects?" I asked as I rinsed out the cups as well and put them in the nearest dish tub.

"That's just part of it." Moose looked at me earnestly as he asked, "Victoria, what if Benny was killed as a direct result of something I said or did?"

The suggestion caught me completely off guard.

"Moose, how could that even be possible?" I asked.

"Think about it. What if someone wanted to kill Benny, but they were afraid that they would be too obvious a suspect in the murder investigation? I might have given them a golden invitation to kill Benny by threatening the man like that in public tonight. If you look at it from that perspective, it might all be my fault."

I could see that the very idea of that was troubling my grandfather greatly. I kissed his cheek gently, and then I said, "Moose, if someone wanted to get rid of Benny, they didn't need your outburst as cover for their crime. It's not your fault."

"Maybe not, but I still don't like it," Moose said.

"Then help me find Benny's killer so we can at least bring the murderer to justice."

"I can do that," Moose said, his mood lightening slightly. "Now, let's get out of here. You've got an early morning tomorrow, and I'm getting up a bit before my usual time as well."

After Moose dropped me off at the house, the porch light flickered once, twice, and then three times. Greg was waiting by the door for me, and I welcomed his embrace as I walked in.

Marrying that man had been one of the best decisions I'd ever made in my life, and while I didn't tell Greg that an awful lot, he knew how I felt.

Chapter 3

"Hey, Mom," I said sleepily the next morning a little before six when I got to the diner. Just as Moose had predicted for himself, I'd had trouble getting to sleep the night before, though I doubted that the coffee had played too much of a role in it. Though my mother had already been there for quite some time getting prepared for that morning's session in the kitchen, she looked wide awake, something I envied greatly at the moment.

"Good morning. Victoria, it appears that your father and I missed quite a bit of excitement at the theater last night, didn't we?" My mother worked the grill every morning until Greg came in at eleven to take over, and I loved the closeness it gave us.

"Do you regret not going?" I asked as I tried to will myself awake. I absently reached up and petted the wooden moose I had stationed above the cash register when I'd first taken the diner over. My grandfather had whittled him for me when I'd been a little girl, and my moose had always been my favorite childhood toy.

"No, with the hours I work, I'm fairly certain that I would have fallen asleep before the curtain went up. I don't know how you do it, Victoria."

"Last night I probably shouldn't have," I said.

Her brow furrowed a bit as she asked, "How bad is it? Is it true that Moose and Martha are the only suspects the sheriff has in Benny's murder?"

"Where did you hear that?" I asked as I started flipping on the main lights of the diner.

"Word gets around fast in Jasper Fork; I shouldn't have to tell you that."

"Well, it's not true. Moose and I managed to come up with four other suspects last night on the spur of the moment."

"Then that must mean that you both are going to investigate this murder, aren't you?"

"We really don't have much choice," I said. "I know you're not a fan of our investigations, but we wouldn't do it if we felt there was any other option."

"I wasn't scolding you, Victoria," my mom said gently. "This time, I don't see that you have much choice in the matter. Just be careful, okay?"

"I promise," I said as I gave my mother a kiss on the cheek.

She smiled at the gesture, and then rubbed her hands together. "In the meantime, we have a diner to run. If you'll excuse me, I need to take the biscuits out of the oven, or we won't have anything to serve our sausage gravy on."

"I'll take the first order myself when they're ready," I said.

"Young lady, did you skip breakfast again?" she asked, the mothering instincts coming out in her voice.

"Why should I have cold cereal at home when I have the best breakfast short-order cook in the state working at my diner?" I asked with a smile.

"Maybe because if you eat my food all of the time, you'll gain twenty pounds in a month," she said. "Besides, cereal is good for you."

"You're seriously not going to cut me off from your sausage and gravy biscuits, are you?"

"Of course not," she said with the hint of a smile. "I'll have your order ready for you in two shakes. There's the morning paper, if you haven't seen it already," she said as she pointed to the slim folded newspaper.

I opened it and scanned the front page, which sported an obituary regaling Benny Booth's theatrical exploits over the years, as well as his success in business. The newspaper hadn't used a headshot from his portfolio for the picture, though. Instead, the photo, front and center in the paper, showed Benny holding his Jasper award. The trophy sported all sorts of fancy filigrees engraved on the cup and delicate wings sculpted into the handles. Silver in color, if not in actual content, it looked a little ostentatious for the caliber of actors it was probably awarded to. Benny was happily embracing it in the shot as though it were vital to his existence.

That was enough of that. I pushed the paper aside, and then I flipped the CLOSED sign to OPEN as I prepared the cash register for the day. By the time I set everything up just the way I liked it, Mom came out of the kitchen with a large plate in her hands. The aroma was unbelievable, and my mouth began to water instantly. She'd managed to bury her luscious golden brown biscuits under an avalanche of sausage gravy, but I didn't mind. I could see a few spots where the butter she'd used on the biscuits had melted and was now part of the gravy's texture. I took a seat at the bar, and after cutting off a healthy bite of biscuit that was laden in gravy, I ate it slowly, enjoying all of the tastes that combined to create a perfect bite. I always said that if I ever lapsed into a coma, they should wave a plate of my mother's sausage gravy biscuits under my nose. If I didn't revive from that, everyone would know that the case would be pretty much hopeless.

"Well, how is it?" Mom asked as she stood by the door that led into the kitchen.

"It's just about the best thing I ever ate in my life," I said, and then to prove it, I took another bite. Wow, it just got better and better. "You *really* need to teach Greg how to do this."

"Your husband's gravy is just fine," Mom said, defending her fellow short order cook.

"His still can't touch yours, as good as it might be, and he knows it just as well as I do," I said.

Mom blushed slightly, but she was clearly pleased with the compliment. I was about to take yet another bite when I heard our front door open. It took real effort on my part to turn away from my breakfast and face our first customer of the day. I was surprised to see Garret Wilkes, a tall, heavyset man with a shock of white hair. What was he doing here? He rarely came into our little diner, and never this early. I had to wonder if the reason he was stopping in at The Charming Moose now had more to do with what had happened last night than with our food, since Garret was the producer *and* director of *The Last Man Left*. For his day job, he ran Wilkes Jewelry, but I knew that theater was where his passion lived.

"Is Moose around, by any chance?" Garret asked me as I approached him with a menu.

"No, he hasn't been in *this* early since he ran the place himself. By the way, I'm sorry about the play last night."

"Unfortunately, these things happen. We're adding another show in two nights and making tonight the play's debut, so we're getting the word out to the community that last night's tickets will be good for either performance on a first come, first serve basis."

"Why skip a night in the middle of your performances?" I asked.

"Unfortunately, the theater was already booked for a magic show before we planned any of this," he said with a frown. "Would you mind if I put a sign up in your window about it?"

Normally I tried to discourage that kind of thing, since it had a tendency to escalate quickly, and before I knew it, I wouldn't be able to see out, but this was different. "How about if we put it up here?" I suggested on the posting board near my wooden moose. "It's near the register, so folks will see it as they pay their bills."

"Yes, but if we put it in the window, they don't even have to eat here to get the news."

I laughed. "Garret, if they don't eat here, I don't really care that much about them in the first place. I'm offering you a prime spot, just this once. Take it or leave it."

"I'll take it," he said with the hint of a smile. "You are as tough a bargainer as your grandfather."

"I'll take that as a compliment. Is that why you wanted to see Moose? You should know that I'm the one who handles things here these days." When my grandfather had first retired, my dad had run the café for a limited amount of time before he'd realized that he hated it, and I'd gladly taken over after that. After all, it was a family business.

"No, this is about something else entirely."

"Just as long as you don't accuse him of what happened to Benny, I'm sure that he'd be glad to talk to you about anything." I saw Garret's face grow a little bit gray when I mentioned the dead actor, so I added, "Garret, here's a piece of friendly advice. Unless you have a death wish, I wouldn't say a word to my grandfather about Benny Booth. If he brings it up first, fine, but I'd leave that up to him if I were you."

"I wasn't going to blame him for the murder," Garret said. "I just wanted to know what Benny said to him at the theater before he died."

"You could always ask me. After all, I was standing right there when they had their confrontation."

Garret's eyes lit up. "What did they talk about?"

"Mostly it was about my grandmother's bottom," I said.

"I heard that rumor, but I thought it was some kind of joke," Garret said.

"Trust me, it was real enough. Evidently, Benny got a little handsy with my grandmother, and understandably, Moose wasn't too happy about it."

"That was just the way Benny was," Garret said. "I told him repeatedly that his overfamiliarity would get him in trouble some day. Moose shouldn't have been so upset with him, though. Benny was mostly harmless. He certainly didn't deserve to die that way."

"Let's get one thing straight. My grandfather was angry with Benny, but he didn't kill him. Moose did not murder your lead actor," I said, fighting to keep my voice calm. "You can take my word on it."

"I never said that he did," Garret answered quickly.

"Maybe not, but the implication was there. I'll say it to you, and to anyone else who needs to hear it; anybody who says that my grandfather killed Benny Booth is a liar."

"I'm truly sorry if I made it sound as if I thought he killed the man," Garret said quickly. "Don't worry. I'm sure that Sheriff Croft will find whoever did it eventually."

"Sure he will," I said. I wasn't about to tell the director that Moose and I were going to do our best to solve the murder case ourselves, but while I had Garret there, I wasn't about to let him leave before he answered a few questions for me. "Speaking of Benny, how did the two of you get along?"

"Well, that's complicated. At times we were best friends," Garret said.

"And at other times?" I asked.

"We fought like crazy," Garret admitted with a smile. "You see, we had artistic differences from time to time, and we each stood firm for what we believed in."

"How bad did the fighting get?"

"What do you mean?" he asked me.

"Were punches ever thrown?"

"Never," he said, looking shocked by the mere suggestion. "Our disagreements were part of our process. There was *never* any personal animosity involved."

"I'm sure there wasn't," I said, though I wasn't, not yet anyway. "Do you know anyone who might have had a *real* beef with Benny?"

"I don't want to spread gossip," the director said.

"I don't know if you've heard it around town, but Moose and I have had a little success in the past tracking down a killer or two."

"Oh, your reputation in the community is the stuff legends are made of," Garret said.

"Well, strictly between the two of us, we've been thinking about looking into Benny's murder ourselves, and you could help us a great deal if you have information that we're not privy to yet."

The director seemed to think about it for a few seconds,

and then Garret said, "I'm sure that you've already heard about his relationship with Sandra Hall."

"They had an actual relationship? I thought she was dating someone else, a young brooding fellow who looks as though he just stepped out of the pages of a fitness magazine."

"That would be Marcus Jackson, but sometimes emotions get confused when actors are performing, especially when the scenes call for assumed familiarity. Benny liked to throw himself into his roles, and from what I saw onstage, at least once Sandra didn't seem to mind his attention."

"But I'm guessing that Marcus did, didn't he?"

Garret frowned. "I ordered a closed set for our rehearsals, but Marcus snuck in, anyway. When he saw Benny kissing Sandra, all perfectly normal and a legitimate part of the scene, he exploded from the back and tried to storm the stage."

"Did he do anything to Benny?" I asked.

"I'm certain that he would have, if I hadn't blocked his way. I used to do a little boxing as a kid, and Marcus never got past me." Garret seemed inordinately proud of his accomplishments as a bouncer at the theater.

"Did he happen to say anything as you were ejecting him?" I asked.

"As a matter of fact, he threatened to make Benny pay for what he'd done," Garret said.

"When did this happen?" I asked.

"It was the day before yesterday, during our final dress rehearsal."

"Have you told the sheriff about it yet?" I asked. I knew that Sheriff Croft would be quite interested to hear what had gone on.

"No, why? Do you think it's important?"

I glanced at the clock, and saw that it was nearing seven. I knew that the sheriff was an early riser, and that he liked to be behind his desk at seven every morning if he had anything to say about it. "I'd advise you to walk over there and tell him what you know right now," I said.

"He's working this early in the morning?" Garret asked.

"Unless I miss my guess he is, and believe me, you don't want him storming into your jewelry shop."

Garret shuddered a little at the thought of that. "No, you're right; it's best if I take care of it right now."

"You probably have time for a little breakfast first, if you'd like," I said, thinking of the diner's bottom line instead of our investigation.

"Thanks, but there's no time for that now. Later, maybe."

"We're open until seven tonight," I said.

After he left, Mom came out of the kitchen. "What was that all about?"

"Garret Wilkes wanted to speak to Moose," I explained as I put the poster up under my wooden moose's position near the register.

Mom laughed. "I'm guessing that he doesn't know that you couldn't blast your grandfather out of bed with dynamite at this time of morning."

"*We* know that, but Garret doesn't. Anyway, I handled it."

"I'm sure that you did," Mom said, and then the front door opened again. Instead of someone there about the murder, though, a group of six men entered, all from a local construction company building a new wing onto our local museum. They made it a habit of eating together at the diner every morning, and I'd grown accustomed to having them there. Ellen rushed over to wait on them, and I told Mom, "Better get ready for a rush of orders. I'm going to go lend her a hand."

"Bring it on. I love cooking for hungry men with big appetites," she said.

"Then, I'd say that you've got the perfect job," I answered. As I helped Ellen pour coffee for our customers, I couldn't help wondering if Garret had been soft-pedaling his own involvement in Benny's murder. After all, he'd even admitted that they'd exchanged heated words recently. Had it all been as harmless as Garret had claimed, or was there a deeper animosity than he was letting on about? As far as I was concerned, the director's name absolutely belonged on our list of suspects until we had a reason to take his name off, and I was glad that he'd stopped in to have a little chat.

Chapter 4

"Victoria, are you ready to go?" Moose asked as he walked into the diner a little before eight, just at the end of my first shift for the day.

"What got *you* out of bed this early?" I asked. We usually *never* saw Moose until the crack of eleven at the earliest.

"We've got people to see," he said. "And the sooner we get started, the quicker I can clear your grandmother's name."

"And yours, too, right?" I asked.

He just shrugged. "Truth be told, I'm not all that worried about my reputation. Unfortunately, your grandmother's skin isn't quite as thick as mine. Martha has been getting some disturbing telephone calls already this morning."

"Who's calling her?"

"You name it, and they've checked in with her, from her sewing circle to her quilters club to her book group. This town is in dire need of something else to talk about besides Benny Booth, if you ask me."

"Murder is a pretty powerful subject matter around here, Moose, but I can't believe that anyone is blaming it on Martha."

"Oh, they aren't doing anything as overt as that, but the questions they're asking her are making her feel like a criminal, and I won't have it."

It was just like my grandfather to care more about my grandmother's reputation in town than it was to have people coming right out and accusing him of murder. He loved her deeply, and I just hoped that when Greg and I were their age, we'd still be going that strong, not that I had any reason to doubt that we would be on just as solid ground. He asked, "Have you had any more ideas since we spoke last night?"

"I've had something quite a bit better than that, actually. I've already had one interesting visitor at the diner this morning. As a matter of fact, he came in here originally looking for you."

"You've got my attention," Moose said. "Who came by?"

"Garret Wilkes popped into the diner not long after we opened."

"What did he want?" my grandfather asked.

"As a matter of fact, the director wanted to talk to you about Benny."

Moose's face clouded up. "The man has some nerve. I suppose that while he was here, he got you to put *that* up," my grandfather said as he gestured to the sign I'd installed.

"Actually, he *wanted* it in the window, but I told him no."

"Good for you," Moose said. "I'm surprised that you even allowed him to put it up there after what happened."

"I can always take it down, if you'd like me to," I said. While it was true that the diner was under my control these days, that didn't mean that I wasn't respectful of Moose's opinions.

"No, leave it right where it is. There are a lot of actors in that play who didn't have anything to do with what happened to Benny last night. There's no use punishing them for what happened. Are you going to the play tonight?"

"I thought I might, if I can get in line soon enough," I said.

"You really do love plays, don't you?"

"Moose, I'm not going for the show," I told him. "I want to talk to the actors about Benny, and what better way of catching them all together than attending one of their performances?"

"What makes you think they'll talk to you?" Moose asked.

"What makes you think they won't?" I asked him in return. "I'm hoping to catch them off-guard."

"It sounds like a good plan. I'm going with you, of

course."

"Do you think that's all that wise?" I asked.

"Why wouldn't it be? After all, *you're* going."

"Yes, but nobody's accusing me of murder this time around, thank the powers that be."

Moose frowned before he said, "Victoria, I *need* to be there with you."

"What if I take Greg as my backup?" I asked. "Would that satisfy you?"

"You're not trying to cut me out of this investigation, are you?" he asked me.

"No, but I don't see any reason to get people up in arms if we can help it, either. How about if I promise to come by your house tonight after the performance and bring you up to speed? Would that help any?"

"I don't suppose that it could hurt," he said. "I still don't like it."

"You realize that I'm not doing it to hurt you, don't you," I asked as I patted his cheek.

"I know you aren't. Victoria, tell Greg that he has to be on his toes tonight. I don't want anything to happen to my favorite granddaughter."

"I'm also your *only* granddaughter, but I appreciate the sentiment, anyway. So, who are we going to talk to in the meantime?"

"You should handle the actors tonight," Moose said, "so that leaves Vern Jeffries, Benny's former business partner, and Marcus Jackson, the jealous boyfriend, for us."

"That sounds good to me," I said. "Do you think we have time to talk to both of them before my next shift starts at eleven?"

"Three hours should give us plenty of time, but if it doesn't, we can always call Martha in to work your lunch shift."

I shook my head. "I'd rather not. How is she going to feel when folks come in and start whispering behind her back? It's happened to me a time or two, and it's not fun, trust me."

"If anyone says one word about her, I'll make them sorry that they were ever born," Moose said angrily.

"Hey, calm down. You're supposed to be turning over a new leaf, remember?"

My grandfather bit his lower lip, and then his expression immediately softened. "You're right. I'm going to do my best for the rest of the day not to threaten anyone."

"I know that it's asking a lot," I said with a grin, "but it would be great if you could follow through with that. So, who do we go see first?"

Moose smiled. "That's a no-brainer. I have no idea how we're going to hunt Marcus Jackson down if he's not at the gym, but I know exactly where Vern Jeffries is."

"How could you possibly know that?" I asked my grandfather.

"I drove by his new office on my way over here, and he's already there at his desk. It's time we paid a little visit to Jeffries Insurance, don't you think?"

"That sounds good to me," I said. "What ruse are we going to use? Are we telling him that we're thinking about changing insurance agencies for the diner?"

Moose shook his head. "No, if we do that, Francie Moore will hear about it, and I don't want her to think that we're leaving her. How about if we shop for a new personal policy for you?"

I thought about the questions that Vern would most likely ask me, including the dreaded one about my current weight, and I killed the idea before my grandfather grew too fond of it. "Let's make it you, instead."

"Why not?" he asked. "I've got nothing to hide."

"Then let's go," I said.

After we were in his truck and driving to Jeffries Insurance, Moose said, "I still can't believe somebody smacked Benny in the back of the head with a statue hard enough to kill him."

"Why not? He certainly made *you* angry enough last

night."

"Victoria, he assaulted your grandmother," Moose said as he voice began to darken. "I would think you'd applaud my reaction."

"I'm sure that Martha could have handled things fine on her own. In a way, when you butted in, you robbed her of the chance to defend her own honor. You realize that, don't you?"

Moose glanced over at me, his skepticism clear in his expression. "What are you talking about, Victoria? This is the South, where men are still allowed to defend the women they love, and I hope they always will be."

"I'm not scolding you, Moose; I'm just trying to show you how your wife might see it. How has she been acting toward you since you jumped to her defense?"

Moose thought about it, and then he said, "She's been a little on edge, but I thought it was because of the man's murder and all."

"The next time you talk to her, ask her how she felt about you coming to her rescue before she had a chance to defend herself. If I'm wrong, I'll buy you dinner."

"On the off chance that you're right, what do I have to buy you?" Moose asked.

"I think the dinner bet stands, but you're going to have to take me to a *much* nicer place than I'm going to take you."

"I don't know, Victoria. I suppose that you *could* be right. The older I get, the more I realize that I still don't know what makes half the human race tick."

"Don't worry. You guys baffle us *almost* as much as we confuse you. That's what keeps things interesting, don't you think?"

"If you say so."

We arrived at the new insurance agency, but instead of going right in, Moose said, "Wait in the truck for one second, would you?"

I knew better than to allow that to happen. "Moose, I can understand it if you're unhappy about me asking you not to go to the theater with me tonight, but that doesn't mean that you can exclude me from interviewing folks from our list of suspects today."

"It's not that," he said. "I just want to call Martha and see if you're right. Not knowing is killing me."

"I'll wait right here, then," I said with a smile.

I watched as Moose paced around in front of the truck, talking with great animation to my grandmother. After two minutes, he hung up, and I took that as a sign that I could get out of the truck, now.

"What did she say?"

"Where would you like to eat?" he asked me. "She was reluctant to admit it at first, but there was a little resentment there, there's no denying it. Victoria, I *still* don't understand how I could have been so wrong about this."

"Don't beat yourself up about it," I said. "Better men than you have failed to understand the women they love."

"Better than *me*? I doubt that man's ever been born," he answered with a grin, and I could feel his charm wash over me. My grandfather had a way about him that appealed to just about everyone, me included. Even when he was contrite, it still showed through. "Let's go talk to Vern, shall we?"

"Lead the way," I said, glad that I had Moose with me, not only as a partner in my investigations, but as my grandfather, too.

Vern Jeffries had a generic looking office that could have housed any one of a dozen different marginal businesses. Seeing him sitting behind his desk, his paunch punishing the buttons of his dress shirt and his bald head gleaming under the fluorescent fixtures, he could have just as easily been an accountant or a child's portrait photographer, for that matter.

"Come in," he said as we approached him. "Moose, I'm glad you called. After I ask you a few questions, we can study our options for your new insurance policy." He glanced at me and added, "Victoria, to be honest with you,

I'm not quite sure why *you're* here. If you'd like to wait in the outer office, we shouldn't be more than half an hour."

"Thanks, but I'll stay here," I said with a bright smile. There was no way that I was going to take one step away from that particular meeting.

Vern looked at me oddly, and then he turned back to Moose. "Are you certain that's okay with you?"

"She's my granddaughter," Moose said as though it was the most natural thing in the world. "Of course she can stay."

"Will Martha be joining us?" Vern asked.

"No, she's tied up elsewhere at the moment." My grandfather was starting to show his impatience with the ruse, so I figured that it was time to start asking our questions before he stormed out.

"Mr. Jeffries, before we get started, we have a few questions for you about your company," I said.

"Go on," Vern said as he sat back in his seat. "I've got nothing to hide."

I sincerely doubted that, but I decided to keep that opinion to myself. "Thank you. We would both appreciate that. First of all, we know that up until recently, you were closely associated with Benny Booth and his firm. Would you mind telling us why you two split up?"

Apparently Vern wasn't as interested in opening up as he'd just implied. "I don't see what that has to do with your grandfather's policy." Vern frowned at me, and then the insurance adjuster asked my grandfather, "Moose, in all the years we've known each other, I've never known you to ever let someone *else* do the talking for you."

"Don't underestimate Victoria," he said. "There's a reason I asked her along. Answer her question. Why should I trust you with my premium money? What happened between you and Benny? I hate to tell you some of the rumors flying around town, especially after what just happened to the man."

"I'm sure that I'm not the only one folks are talking about," Vern said.

That was a direct dig at Moose, but I couldn't afford to let my grandfather respond to it, not if I wanted to get any information about Benny from Vern. "We can appreciate that," I said, "but we need to know a little about your past before we can invest any of our future with you."

Moose started to add something, but I could see him bite the remark back.

Vern shrugged, and then he threw his pen down on his desk. "Yes, it's true that Benny and I ran an agency together for sixteen months. It was a mistake, something I realized as soon as we got started, but how big a mistake it was I'm just beginning to find out."

"In what way?" I asked.

"I hate to speak ill of the dead, but the man had a way of making money vanish that still confounds me. It wouldn't surprise me if they have to screw him into the ground; he was that crooked. Does that answer your question?"

"Where does that leave you, besides bitter towards him?" I asked.

"Of course I'm bitter. He took something good of mine and ruined it for his own benefit. Now I'm picking up the pieces and trying to start over again."

"It sounds as though you had quite a grudge against him," Moose said.

"I'm not denying that I did, but the last thing I wanted to happen was for someone to kill him."

"Would you mind explaining that?" I asked him.

Vern took in a deep breath, and then he let it out slowly before he spoke again. "While Benny was still alive, I had a chance, no matter how slim it was, to get my money back. With him gone, the money's lost as well."

"How much are we talking about here?" Moose asked.

"Six figures, at least," Vern said.

"Just out of curiosity, where were you last night when it happened?" I asked.

"I was the same place that I've been every night since I went out on my own; I was here behind my desk, trying to figure out how I'm going to make this business a success. So far, I'm not having much luck." He reached forward, moved his pen, and then closed the open folder on his desk. "I'm guessing this meeting is over."

"What makes you think that?" I asked.

"It's obvious you came in here to ask me about Benny. You never were interested in a new insurance policy, were you? At least not from me, at any rate. I'm not even saying that I blame you. I'm too old to start from scratch again."

"We *might* be interested," Moose said.

"If that's true, call me later for an appointment, and we'll discuss it. I'm just not in the mood to deal with this anymore today."

"Thanks for your time," I said as we all stood.

"You're welcome to it, for whatever it was worth. For the record, I hope you figure out who did it."

"What are you talking about?" I asked as innocently as I could manage.

For the first time since we'd come into his office, Vern Jeffries actually smiled. "You're investigating Benny's death, and I don't blame you. Moose, you must be feeling the heat pretty solidly right now, but if it helps any, you aren't alone. The sheriff's already been here grilling me, so I'm not surprised that you're in the thick of it, too. I'll tell you what I told him. If you really want to know who killed Benny, you should look at his ex, Amanda Lark. She could scare the label off a paint can, and from what *I* saw, he was terrified of her, and that's when they were getting along. After he dumped her, I heard that she threatened to come after him with a butcher knife."

"Do you happen to know where we might find her?" I asked.

"The last I heard, she was working at Mad Dog; you know, the furniture outlet on the edge of town. Watch yourself around that woman. She bites."

"We'll be careful," Moose said. "Thanks for the information. We'll see you later."

"Have your people call my people," Vern said with a hollow laugh. "Except I don't have people, at least not anymore. Now, if you two will excuse me, I'm going to lock my front door and get stinking drunk. I don't care how early in the day it is. You're both free to join me, but I should warn you, I get a little morose after I've had a few."

"Maybe next time," Moose said as Vern walked us out.

Once we were through the door, he closed it and locked it behind us, pulling the shade with one hand as he waved good-bye to us with the other.

"What do you make of that?" I asked Moose.

"I think the man needs to be on a suicide watch," he said.

"Do you really think that he'd do something that drastic?"

"I don't know, but I'm going to make a few telephone calls to see if I can find a single friend he has left. Vern shouldn't be alone right now, in my opinion."

I was starting to really worry now. "Should I go back in and keep him company while you're on the phone?"

"I doubt he'd open the door for us again, but when I was digging around earlier, I heard about one man who might be able to lend us a hand."

Moose made his call while I stared at Vern Jeffries' office door. What was he doing behind that pulled shade? Should we have left him alone?

After a brief chat, Moose hung up the phone. "It's good. Steve Pierce will be here in five minutes."

"You called the man's *barber*?" I asked. Steve was a good guy, and he liked to eat some of his meals with us at the diner.

"They're fishing buddies. It was the best I could do, Victoria. Anyway, he's coming right over."

"We're waiting here, aren't we?" I asked.

"If you don't mind," he said.

"I'm happy to do it," I replied.

Steve got there soon enough, a barber as bald as the day he was born. "How bad is he?"

"He's probably already cracked his first bottle by now, if that gives you any indication," Moose said.

"Thanks for calling me. I know that Vern's not a ray of sunshine on his best day, but he's a good man to have in your corner when you're down. That's what nearly killed him about this deal with Benny. That man took advantage of Vern's good nature, and he walked all over him. Now, let me see if I can get him to answer the front door. No offense, but it might be easier if you two were gone, if you know what I mean."

"Happy to do it. Thanks again for coming."

"Hey, if something happens to Vern, who am I going to go fishing with?" Steve asked with a grin.

Moose drove off, but before he could get far, he pulled into a lot a few doors down so we could see what was going on.

"I was just about to suggest that you pull over," I said.

"Great minds think alike," Moose said with a slight grin.

We both watched in silence as Steve repeatedly knocked on the door, to no avail. I was about to suggest that we call 911 when the shade finally came up and Vern opened the door. After a brief conversation, the insurance agent moved to one side, opened the door, and the barber walked in.

"That's a relief," I said.

"Honestly, it's a short-term patch, but it's all we can do. What do you say? Are you ready to go after our next suspect?"

"I'm game if you are."

"Good. Then, if it were up to me, I'd say we go to Mad Dog Furniture and find Amanda."

"Why not? This just gets better and better, doesn't it?" I asked as Moose pulled back out onto the road and drove toward the edge of town.

"It's not the life of glamour they make investigating look like on television, but then again, what is?" he asked. "At least we get to nose around and ask a lot of impertinent questions."

"After what Vern told us, I'm not entirely certain that it's a good thing hearing their answers, though," I said.

"Cheer up. After all, how much worse could it get?"

"Do you really want to hear my answer to that question?" I asked Moose.

"On second thought, I'll pass. Hopefully we'll get a little more from Amanda than we were able to get out of Vern."

"That's what I'm afraid of," I said. "I've heard some pretty scary stuff about the woman."

"I'm sure that she's not as bad as folks make her out to be," Moose said.

"I guess we'll find out soon enough, won't we?"

Chapter 5

I hadn't been to the furniture outlet in years, and in the time since my last visit, the place had gotten seedier and more rundown than I could have imagined. What would possess someone to shop there, let alone come to work there every day? The signage had long ago faded from its original bright colors, and muted flags hung limp from the awnings, which were covered with leaves. One of the concrete steps had a corner knocked off, and there were cracks all through the thing. I wasn't sure the steps were safe to walk up, and honestly, the building wasn't much better.

I steeled myself for what was inside, and I held my breath as Moose and I walked through the front door. The first thing I noticed was the canned music coming out tinny from the loudspeakers. A handful of customers browsed throughout the expanse of cheap furniture, wandering around a little like zombies in the flickering overhead lights.

If I had to work there five days a week, I'd stick a fork in the nearest electrical outlet and be done with it.

There was no sales staff on the floor, at least none that I could see, but there were a few folks hanging around the sales counter in the middle of the store.

"Can I help you find something?" a middle-aged woman with a lipstick-stained smile asked us as we approached.

"I hope so. We're looking for Amanda Lark," Moose said.

"Well, you've found her, sweetheart. May I ask who recommended me?"

"Vern Jeffries," I answered without thinking.

The smile vanished instantly. "What did that weasel want?"

"He told us that you weren't too happy about your break up with Benny Booth," I said.

"Is he still spreading lies about Benny and me? We ended things like a couple of adults do, with a kiss on the cheek and a smile. The problem with Vern is that he never got over the fact that I turned him down to go out with Benny."

"When did that happen?" I asked.

"When do you think? Listen, if you're not here to look at furniture, sorry, I don't have time for you."

"Yes, I can see that you're overwhelmed with customers at the moment," Moose said.

She was about to answer when I decided that a little peacemaking might be in order. "Actually, my husband has been talking about getting a big sectional couch," I said. "Would you mind showing me what you've got?"

"Sure, why not? You and your husband just follow me," she said.

"He's not my *husband*," I said. "This is my grandfather."

Moose quickly added, "Not that I couldn't land a young lady for myself if I were in the market for one."

"Sure, sure. Whatever. It takes all kinds."

"Even though you were broken up, you must have been devastated when you heard about Benny's murder," I said as we started moving through the store.

"It was quite a shock," Amanda said.

"Where were you when it happened?" I asked her.

"I was… hang on. Why should *you* care where I was?"

I hadn't expected her to balk so quickly, so I had to come up with something on the fly. I said the first thing that came to mind, and I hoped that it would work. "I just wanted to know if you felt anything, like a psychic tug, when Benny was murdered. What *were* you doing at the time he died, do you know?"

"I was busy away from the theater having a life, and no, I didn't feel a thing."

"Nothing at all?" Moose asked.

I shot my grandfather a warning look. Was he trying to antagonize this woman? Before she could react, I quickly asked Amanda, "How long did you and Benny date?"

"It was a while," she said. "As a matter of fact, he was still in business with Vern, if that gives you any idea."

"We were wondering what made them end their ties," I asked. "Do you have any idea what happened between them?"

"Sure. Vern thought he was the shark, only it turned out that he was wrong. Benny got the best of him, and Vern wouldn't take it like a man, so he took all of his marbles and went home."

"Is that what happened with you and Benny?" Moose asked. "Did he get the better of you, too?"

"I told you, our breakup was mutual," Amanda said heatedly.

"That's not the way I heard it," Moose said.

"Moose," I snapped.

"Hey, I'm just saying out loud what everyone else is thinking," my grandfather said.

Amanda looked at him coldly, and then she called out, "Hey, Reggie. Come here."

I looked over to see a large man lumbering over our way. He looked to be a real bruiser, and I wondered if they employed him to move large furniture all by himself. From his size, I doubted it would be that much of a problem for him.

"What's up, Amanda?" he asked.

"These two need help finding their way out," she said.

"Let's go. Follow me; it's this way," Reggie said.

Moose didn't look as though he wanted to budge, but I tugged at his arm. "That's not a bad idea. I'll bring my husband back later. Maybe you could show us something then."

"Leave this one at home, and I'd be happy to help you any way that I can," Amanda said.

"Come on," Reggie said a little impatiently. "I don't have all day."

"Let's go, Moose," I whispered, and he finally agreed.

After we were outside, I asked, "What were you thinking? You really went after Amanda in there."

"She wasn't going to answer our questions unless we got her off-balance," he said. "I decided to push her a little and see what happened."

"What happened is that we got thrown out of the store," I said.

"At least we got a reaction," Moose said. "I don't know about you, but I'm not buying the 'gentle breakup' routine."

"It doesn't really match her style, does it?"

"Not a chance," he said. "At least she confirmed that Vern has a motive for killing Benny."

"I'll have to ask her more the next time I come back. I hope I can convince Greg to come with me. You know how he hates to shop."

"I'm happy to come back with you," Moose said. "She'll get over it by the time we get here next time."

"What if she doesn't? Moose, we need to be able to interview our suspects without alienating them."

"Sorry, I just thought a little direct action was called for."

It didn't do any good scolding him, partly because there were times when his direct approach was perfect. "Don't worry. We'll find another way to tackle her." I glanced at my watch. "Well, since that took a lot less time than I thought it might, we've still got time to tackle Marcus Jackson. What do you say? Do you feel like going to the gym?"

"As long as I don't have to do a workout, I'm all for it," Moose said as we got back into his truck and took off.

I grinned at him. "You never know. A little exercise might just do you some good."

"Or it could kill me. Frankly, I'm not willing to take the chance. I get all of the exercise I need walking, thank you very much. I don't need a machine to get a decent workout."

"I don't know. I've often thought that it might be nice joining a gym," I said.

"When would you have time?" he asked.

"You've got a point, but let's not tell anyone there about my schedule at the diner. The only way we're going to get anyone to talk to us is if I pretend I'm about to sign up."

"I'll keep quiet," Moose said.

I raised one eyebrow, but I didn't say a word.

"What? Don't you believe I can keep my mouth shut if I want to?" my grandfather asked.

"I believe that you *can*," I said with a smile. "I'm just not sure that you *will*."

"Just watch me," Moose answered.

We walked into the gym, and I was amazed by the wide variety of exercise equipment they had there. On the right, there were rows and rows of treadmills, about half of them currently occupied, and nearby there were a dozen elliptical machines. Only one of them was in use, and I had to wonder if it might be a harder exercise than simply walking or running. On the left, there were pieces of equipment that I couldn't even guess how to use, or even know exactly what they were supposed to do. In the rear of the large room was a wall full of mirrors, along with free weights that were being ignored. The attire of the people there ranged from shiny spandex to cotton sweatpants and sweatshirts, and it was pretty easy to see who had come for a workout, and who had come fishing for some attention. A fit man wearing a polyester track suit approached us with a smile the second he noticed us, and I saw by his badge that his name was Marcus. To my knowledge, he'd never been in our diner, but to be fair, this was the first time that I'd ever stepped inside his gym.

"Hello," he said warmly. "Are you here in response to our ad in the paper?"

"I am," I said.

"How about you, sir?" he asked Moose.

"I'm just along for the ride," my grandfather said.

"I can assure you, we have a great many members in your age range here. They mostly come in later in the day, though."

"I'm sure that they do," Moose said. "For now, though, we're here for her."

"I'd be glad to answer any questions you might have about our facilities. It's important to know that we have men and women trainers, so if you'd be more comfortable with a woman, I can highly recommend Sandra to help you."

"Does she happen to be here at the moment?" I asked. I had my own reasons for asking. I didn't want the amateur thespian seeing me interview her boyfriend.

"No, she's off for the next three days because of the play she's in, but she'll be back in four days after they wrap it all up."

"You seem to know her schedule pretty well," I said. "Are you two an item, by any chance?"

"We've been dating for a while, yes," Marcus said with an easy smile. "The gym is a handy place to meet members of the opposite sex."

"Oh, I'm already married," I said as I waved my ring at him.

"Me, too," Moose said.

"Did you just say that she's in a play?" I asked as innocently as I could manage. "That's where that man was murdered last night, wasn't it? Do you know anything about what happened to him?"

"Just what's in the paper," Marcus said, but it was clear that he wasn't in any mood to talk about Benny. That was too bad, because I wasn't about to just let it go, since it was the real reason I was there.

"Hang on a second," I said as though the information was just dawning on me. "Your girlfriend isn't playing the lead, is she? Funny, I heard that she had something going on with the lead actor behind the scenes, if you know what I mean."

"That's nonsense. I hate it when people spread rumors, especially when they aren't true," Marcus said, suddenly having a more difficult time keeping his smile front and center. "We're open from six am until nine pm every day, so I'm sure we can make your schedule work here. Would you like to take a tour of the facilities? I can personally show you how to use each machine in order to get the maximum benefit from it."

"In a minute," I said. The last thing I wanted to do was watch Marcus Jackson exercise while Moose and I watched him. "I'd like to hear more about the play. Where were you when that unfortunate man was murdered?"

"Why should you possibly care about that?" Marcus asked. "That's exactly what the sheriff wanted to know last night."

"What did you tell him?" I asked.

"Listen, I'm afraid that we've gotten off-track here. Our memberships are refundable on a prorated basis if you find that you're unhappy with your decision, but I can assure you that you won't be. When people join our gym, they tend to stay. I'd be happy to talk to you about what we have to offer here, but I'm not all that comfortable answering any other questions."

"That's a shame," I said. "I was kind of hoping that this was a friendlier place than that. Don't people like to talk about anything *besides* working out?"

He *had* to be working on commission signing new members, because Marcus's tone changed instantly. "Of course we do. It's just that the play is difficult to talk about, given what happened."

"I don't know why you won't tell her where you were when it happened," Moose asked. "It's not like she's accusing you of anything. Is there something that you're hiding?"

"If you must know, I was backstage in Sandra's dressing room," he said. "She was nervous before her big performance, and she wanted me nearby."

"Were the two of you together the whole time?" I asked.

"No. She had a bad case of nerves, so she spent quite a bit of time in the restroom. Unfortunately, she doesn't have one in her dressing room, so she was down the hall most of the time."

"Are you saying that you just sat there alone and waited for her?" I asked.

"What else could I do? I'm a loyal boyfriend," he said. "Now, what do you think about our gym? I can assure you that it's the best in the region."

I was about to ask him another question when a middle-aged woman cramming too much body into too little spandex approached us. In a cloying voice, she asked, "Marcus, could you show me how to use this machine again? I can't seem to get the knack of it."

"I'd be glad to, Mrs. Nance, but I'm with some guests right now."

I doubted that Marcus was going to answer too many more questions, and I needed to get out of there before he managed to talk me into joining. "Why don't you go ahead and help her? I'll take a brochure and think about it. Who knows? I may come back later and talk to Sandra herself."

"About the gym, right?"

"Of course," I said, and then turned to my grandfather. "Are you ready?"

"I am," he said, and we walked out of the gym with Marcus watching us in clear frustration. He thought he'd had a live one on the hook, but I was going to slip away before I signed anything.

Once we were back outside and in my grandfather's truck driving away from the gym, Moose said, "The man's kind of persuasive, isn't he? I thought he had you there for a second."

"Just because I don't act in any community theater productions doesn't mean that I can't be convincing when I want to be. Marcus has no alibi for the murder, does he?"

"He said he was waiting for Sandra in her dressing room," Moose said.

"He admitted that he was alone, though, so there's no way to prove it one way or the other. How hard would it be for him to slip next door, kill Benny, and then get back to Sandra's dressing room before anyone noticed that he was gone?"

"But the sheriff said that Benny's outside door was unlocked."

"Then I'd say that Marcus was pretty smart to open it after he killed Benny. What better way to divert suspicion away from himself than to open that door as he was leaving? No one thinks the murder was committed by someone inside with that door found unlocked."

"He was still taking a chance," Moose said. "Sandra could have come back in at any second, and then where would he be?"

"I just had another thought," I said. "What if Sandra did it herself? She claimed to be in the bathroom, but who would notice the leading lady walking down the hall toward Benny's dressing room? She could have killed him, and then walked back to the bathroom without anyone knowing what she'd just done."

"So, neither one of them has an alibi, so they both need to stay on our list," Moose said. "Why don't we ever get an easy murder to solve?" my grandfather asked me.

"Because if it was truly simple, the sheriff could solve it without any help from either one of us. At least we've got alibis for some of the people we've talked to so far."

Moose just shrugged. "Sure, but I'm not sure what they're worth. Vern claims that he was at his office, alone. Amanda was busy, whatever that means, and I have to assume that she was alone as well, or most likely she would have told us. Marcus just admitted that he was alone in Sandra's dressing room, and evidently Sandra was by herself in the bathroom. Not a single one of these alibis can be confirmed by *anyone*. It's not much, if you ask me."

"Don't get discouraged, Moose. We're just getting started."

"I know that, but you have to admit that it would be nice to be able to eliminate *one* of our suspects early on in our investigation."

"What fun would that be?" I said as I looked at my

watch. It was nearly eleven, and I was due back at work soon. "I'm sorry to be a party-pooper, but I need to get back to the diner. My next shift is getting set to start."

"I could always call Martha and have her cover it for you."

"Thanks, but I wouldn't know what to do or who to talk to, even if we *had* more time. I need some time to think about what we've learned so far, and it wouldn't hurt you to ponder a little, either."

"Sure, that's fine. I understand."

My grandfather was giving in way too easily. What was he up to? "Moose, what are you going to do once I get back to work? You're not going to hunt down any of our other suspects, are you?"

"You're the one freelancing at the theater tonight without me," Moose said.

"That's because you've already worn out your welcome with Garret Wilkes. Besides, I promised that I'd report to you as soon as I'm finished tonight. Promise me that you won't get yourself into any trouble."

He grinned that famous grin of his before he said, "Victoria, don't make me promise something I might not be able to deliver." He stopped in front of The Charming Moose and said, "Now, hop out or you're going to be late."

I didn't have much choice but to do what he asked. Besides, Greg was inside starting his own shift at the diner, and I wanted a chance to say hello to him before I had to get started on my next five-hour stint working the floor as a waitress, cashier, and hostess. Chances were, that wouldn't leave me much time to think about what we'd learned so far, but that was fine with me. Being busy helping customers would allow my subconscious to keep churning away on our murder investigation.

At least that was the plan.

Chapter 6

"Hey there, stranger," Greg said as he wrapped me up in a hug before I could get into the kitchen. "I wasn't sure you were going to make it back in time for your shift."

"You should know me better than that. I haven't been late in donkey years," I said as I laughed and pushed him away. After I glanced at the clock, I said, "Shouldn't you be manning the grill now?"

"I have one minute left," Greg answered with a smile. "Besides, your mom won't mind if I'm a minute or two late, not if I'm kissing you."

Sometimes my husband got in a playful mood, and far be it from me to stop him, but I also didn't want to have this exchange in front of our paying customers. "You're not getting a kiss until we're in the kitchen."

"I'll race you, then," he said as he hurried to the back.

He beat me, but not by much. As I went through the door, he kissed me soundly, and my mother started applauding. Greg was clearly embarrassed by her display, but I took time to curtsy.

"It's good to see young people in love," Mom said.

"I think it's good to see *anybody* feeling that way," I countered.

"Agreed." She turned to Greg as she added, "If you'd like a little more time to romance my daughter, I'd be glad to keep working the grill."

"No, thanks; I've got it," he said.

"Then I think I'll go pay a visit to your father at work. You two have inspired me," she said with a grin as she hung her apron up.

"What got into you?" I asked Greg after Mom was gone and we had the kitchen to ourselves.

"Can't a man show his wife a little affection?" Greg asked.

"Of course he can, but he usually doesn't, at least not while they're both at work."

"What can I say? Murder makes me realize how fleeting our grasp on life is sometimes, you know? I'd hate to ever lose you, Victoria."

"I'll do my best to stay found, then," I said as I touched his cheek lightly.

Mom popped her head back in for a second. "I hate to interrupt, but Ellen needs you out on the floor, Victoria."

"Duty calls," I said, and I walked her out the door.

After Mom was gone, I smiled at Ellen and then I got busy working. Mom had been right. We were having an early lunch rush, and it was going to take both Ellen *and* me to feed these hungry folks.

I was ringing up a customer later when our front door opened. As I looked up, a father somewhere in his late twenties and his five-year-old son walked into the diner together. That in and of itself wasn't all that odd, except for the fact that they were both wearing bright red super-hero capes. I fought to hide my grin as I gave my customer his change, and then I grabbed a couple of menus and headed over to the dynamic duo.

Sliding the menus in front of them, I asked, "Having a good day so far?"

The dad smiled, while his son grinned from ear to ear.

"We're out fighting crime," the boy said.

Dad nodded. "And building shelves in Tommy's room, too."

"Whose room?" the little boy asked his dad.

"Sorry. Super Dude's secret hideaway."

The boy poked a thumb toward his chest, which sported an SD logo that was obviously homemade with love. "That's me, but don't tell anybody that my real name is Tommy."

I locked my lips with an imaginary key. "Your secret is safe with me."

He lowered his voice as he looked around and asked

solemnly, "Do you have any bad guys here we need to take care of?"

I looked around as well, pretending to size up my customers. "No, at the moment, I believe that we're safe."

"If any of them come in, tell us and we'll take care of them. Right, Dad?"

"Right, Super Dude," Dad said. "In the meantime, could we have two grilled cheese sandwiches, two bowls of tomato soup, and two glasses of milk, please?"

"Coming right up," I said as I took their order to Greg directly.

As I walked into the kitchen, my husband was standing near the pass-through window grinning at me. "Why do I feel so safe all of a sudden?" he asked me.

"You saw them, too? I think that guy's father of the year."

"I do, too." Greg took the order, and I delivered the milk. After a few minutes, their order was ready, and as I reached for the plates, I saw that my husband had done his best to carve the Super Dude logo into each sandwich.

I winked at him through the window, and then I delivered everything to the father and son team. "Here you go, specially made just for you from our kitchen."

Tommy nodded, and then he saw his logo emblazoned on his sandwich. He grabbed his father's arm and asked excitedly, "Dad, did you see this? How cool is that?"

The father smiled. "It's very cool." He looked at me and mouthed the words, 'Thank you,' and I nodded back with a smile.

It did my heart good seeing that kind of bond between father and son.

"Fancy seeing you here, Fred," I said as the understudy walked into the diner a little later. He was an average man in just about everyway you could describe him. Average height and weight, Fred's hair and eye colors were both brown. I'd known the man most of my life, but if I had to pick him out of a lineup, I wasn't sure that I could do it. "I can't remember the last time I saw you eating here."

"I agree. It's been too long," he said.

"How are your car dealerships going?"

"We're still in business, so I can't complain," he answered with a grin. I knew that Fred did well for himself, despite the poormouthing.

"What can I get for you?" I asked him.

"I'd love a glass of your sweet tea, and if you don't mind, I could use some information, too," he said with a practiced smile.

"Well, we've got plenty of tea, but I'm not sure how much news I've got to share with you. What did you have in mind?"

"I was kind of wondering if you'd had any luck figuring out who killed Benny yet," he said in a soft voice.

"What makes you think that I'm looking into that?" I asked.

He laughed richly. "Victoria, your reputation as a crime solver goes beyond these four walls. The entire town knows what you and your grandfather do, and since he's tied in so directly with this case, you're bound to be doing a little investigation work on your own, so don't bother denying it."

"It's true that we might have asked a question here and there," I admitted, "but nothing we do is ever official. To be honest with you, I'm a little surprised that you're not more curious about what happened to Benny yourself. It took you long enough to come around today."

"What can I say? I've been busy," the car dealership owner said as he took a healthy swallow of sweet tea. "I believe that I'm just curious enough about what happened to him. Benny and I weren't exactly friends, but we weren't enemies, either. Why should I get more involved than I am?"

"Come on. You can't be surprised by the fact that you're probably on everybody's suspect list."

"No, I suppose that I expected as much. Does that include your list as well?" he asked with the hint of a smile.

"You'd better believe it," I said.

The smile faltered a little, and then Fred said, "Victoria, I'm disappointed in you."

"Are you? I can't even begin to list the things *I'm* disappointed in. Fred, *you* own a pair of car dealerships. Let me ask you something. Where's my rocket car? I read science fiction growing up. Just about everybody led me to believe that by now I'd be scooting around in a rocket car, so what I want to know is, where's mine?"

"It's not under my area of responsibility," he said with a weakened grin. "I'd like to know something, Victoria. Why am I really on your list? I'm no killer."

"According to something that I once read, we all are, if we're backed far enough into a corner, or if we want something badly enough."

Fred said officiously, "There's nothing that I want, or anything that I'm afraid of."

"Wow, it must be terrific being you. Seriously, how did you manage that?"

He was clearly puzzled by the direction our conversation had taken. "We're getting off-topic here. I asked you a question, and I'd really like an answer."

"Okay," I said, "you asked for it. Fred, everyone in seven counties knows that you wanted the lead in that play. It must have crushed you when Benny got it."

He shook his head. "Sure, I thought that I'd be good doing it, but do you really think that I'm that petty, that I'd kill someone for a part in a *community theater* play?"

"I'm sure that people have been murdered for less," I said.

"Maybe so, but nobody that I've ever known. My competition is tough, but they aren't that tough. Sure, we all talk a mean game, but that's all it is, just talk."

"Fred, when was the last time you saw Benny alive?"

He pursed his lips, and after a moment or two, the car dealer said, "It had to be when we were all backstage before the show. I saw him, along with a dozen other cast-mates.

From the sheer logistics of it I couldn't have done it. I heard that whoever killed him came in from the outside."

"That's just one theory," I said. "I believe that the murderer could have just as easily done it by slipping in from the hallway, killing Benny, and then unlocking the outside door before escaping back into the anonymity of the backstage crowd."

"Victoria, how many people do you think are backstage before a performance?" he asked me.

"After reading the playbill, I know that there had to be at least a dozen."

"More than that, actually, when you count the crew. The only problem is that you're forgetting something," Fred said. "We all know each other. Don't you think that if someone had tried to slip in and out of Benny's dressing room someone would have seen them?"

"You folks are good at disguises, though, aren't you?"

"Are you talking about our wardrobes?" Fred asked. "We had several dress rehearsals before Garret thought we were good enough to put the show on. I know the cast in their street clothes as well as their costumes."

"You probably do," I said, "but what if they were wearing *another* type of disguise?" I was playing this interrogation by the seat of my pants, but the question was valid nonetheless. Moose and I needed to broaden our investigation to not just the actors and crew, but to anyone else who might have slipped backstage to commit the murder in disguise. Instead of eliminating suspects, I was doing a fine job of adding a *bunch* more possibilities to our list.

"Victoria, all of this speculation on your part is useless. Have you and your grandfather made any *real* progress on the case?"

I decided to tell the truth. "Not that we've been able to tell so far," I said.

"That's a pity," he said.

It was time to change the subject. "Are you taking Benny's place tonight?" I asked.

"I am. You know what they say," Fred answered. "The show must go on."

"That's sure what it looks like," I said.

"If you need any help, all you have to do is ask," he said.

"Thanks, but I doubt that you can help us, unless you know who killed Benny."

"Sorry. I can't help you there."

"Then there's nothing you can do," I said.

Fred shook his head, and without another word, he slipped two singles onto the counter and left.

I got the distinct impression that he wasn't too happy about the way our conversation had just gone.

Well, that was just too bad. If Moose and I were going to have any luck at all solving Benny's murder, then we were going to have to stir the pot a little, and if we happened to offend a few folks along the way, that was just something we were going to have to live with.

I doubted that we'd see Fred Hitchings at The Charming Moose again anytime soon. Something we'd discussed made me wonder, though.

How hard would it be to slip backstage before the play started? Tonight, I was going to find out, and I might just bring a prop of my own to help.

I thought about going home and grabbing a quick nap on my next break at four, but I just had an hour, and after making the commute, I had even less time than that to snooze. Ultimately I decided to brave it out, stick around, and join my husband in the back, something I did more often than not most days.

"What sounds good this evening?" I asked as I walked back to the kitchen to see him.

Greg smiled at me. "I was hoping you'd ask me that. What do you think about blowing off the play, going home, and kicking our feet up? I can't remember the last time we sat around and just did nothing."

"I was talking about something to eat," I said.

"I wasn't. Don't worry. I'll feed you before we leave, Victoria. Just don't drag me back to that playhouse again."

"Last night hardly counted, since you never actually saw anyone perform," I said as I tweaked his cheek. "You worry too much. It's going to be fun."

"I don't see how, but I'll take your word for it." Greg turned back to the grill, rubbed his hands together, and then he said, "I could always grill us up a couple of plain hamburgers. How does that sound?"

"Greg, there's nothing plain about your burgers, and you know it." I thought about eating such a heavy meal, knowing how Greg liked to pile on the toppings. "On second thought, eggs might be nice." I knew that some places stopped serving breakfast at eleven, but not us. If we were open, eggs were always on the menu.

"That could be fun," he said. "Would you like scrambled?"

"Sure, why not? Throw in a little chopped bacon along with it while you're at it."

"And some cheese," Greg said. "Some mozzarella would go great in that. How about some bell peppers, too?"

"Hang on. I don't want a full-blown omelet," I said.

"Put yourself in my hands," Greg said. "Besides, this is going to be for both of us, so I should get a little input, too, shouldn't I?"

"Go on. Make whatever you'd like to. I'm sure that it will be delicious," I said, knowing that was his plan anyway. I could cook, but nowhere near as well as Greg could, and we both knew it. While Mom could outshine my father in the kitchen, Moose was better at it than Martha ever was. If I ever had a daughter, I hoped that she'd be able to outcook any man in her life, and if I knew Greg, he'd make sure of it.

"That's the spirit," he said as he gave me a quick kiss, and then my husband promptly forgot all about me. When Greg was at his station at the grill, he showed remarkable focus. I'd learned early on not to engage him in conversation while he was focused on cooking, since it was doubtful that he'd remember a word of what we'd said.

"I might as well glance at our inventory and see where we stand while I've got a little time on my hands," I said.

"Why don't you just take a break, Victoria? You're supposed to be off right now, remember?"

"Honestly, Greg, do I ever *really* have any downtime?" I asked.

"You do now. Grab us something to drink and set a place at the table. Our meal will be finished in a dash." I was about to protest when he said with a grin, "Don't argue with the chef."

"No, Sir," I said as I echoed his smile. "How does chocolate milk sound to drink?"

"What are you having?" he asked.

"Chocolate milk," I answered.

"Then make it two," he said.

"Dinner is served," he said a minute later as he neatly divided the huge omelet and plated both sections.

"I can't eat all of this," I said. What I had on my plate alone was enough for three people.

"You underestimate your appetite," he said. "Go on and take a bite, and then tell me you don't have room for all of it."

I knew better than to argue. I did as he told me, and then I felt the ambrosia strike my palate, and smiled. The cheeses blended together perfectly, and matched the subtle and varied hues of the mushrooms, bacon, and bell peppers. They combined into something greater than their parts, and I decided to stop protesting and start eating.

Sometimes I hated it when Greg was right. Not only did I polish off my portion of our omelet dinner, but I probably could have eaten a little bit of his, if any had been left.

"That was magnificent," I said as I put my napkin down on the empty plate. "Thank you."

"You're most welcome. Do you have any room for dessert?"

I groaned a little at the mere thought of it. "Sorry, but I

couldn't eat another bite."

"Even if your mother brought some banana pudding over while you were gone?"

It was my favorite dessert ever, and Greg knew it. At Christmases, Martha had made a small bowl of it just for me, and no one was allowed to sample from my bowl, not even Moose. Mom had carried on the tradition at the diner. Whenever she made banana pudding, there was always a small bowl set aside just for me.

Sometimes it was great working where I did.

"Maybe I could have one bite," I said, though I wasn't at all sure where I was going to put it.

"Should I grab two spoons?" Greg asked. "I'd be more than happy to help you with it."

"You can if you'd like, but you're not getting any of my banana pudding, so don't even ask."

"What happened to us sharing everything once we got married?" he asked me with that grin of his that never failed to lighten my heart.

"I told you then, and I'll tell you now. There's a great many things that I'll share with you, but banana pudding is not one of them."

He threw a rag at me. "Suit yourself. I'll just get mine out of the common bowl."

"That works out great for me."

I only meant to take a bite or two, but I was halfway through the bowl when Greg asked, "We're still going tonight, right?"

"We are," I said as I finished the bite on my spoon.

"And are you still planning to wear the same dress you wore last night?"

"I thought I would, since it's the best one that I own."

He lifted up a cookie sheet and held in front of him as a shield as he said, "Then, you might want to give that dessert a rest if you have any hope of fitting back into it."

He flinched, as though preparing himself for an assault, but I didn't throw anything. Instead, I put my spoon in one of the dirty dish bins, wrapped the pudding up, and then I put it back in the fridge on a tall shelf in back. "Thanks for that," I said.

"I should be the one thanking you," he said.

"Why is that?"

"You let me get away with saying that without throwing a single thing in my direction. Your restraint is growing by leaps and bounds."

I kissed his cheek. "I appreciate the sentiment, but let's not make a habit of it," I said with a smile. After glancing at the clock, I said, "I'm going on out early to help Jenny. We've got a little more than two hours here, and then we get to go home and get ready for the play again."

"I just hope that it has a better ending tonight," Greg said, and then he caught himself. "That wasn't the best thing in the world that I could have said, was it?"

"That's why you work in the kitchen away from our customers," I said with a laugh.

"Yeah, when you think about it, that's probably a good thing. At least nobody's going to die at the theater tonight."

"That's my hope, too, but I'm not making any promises."

Chapter 7

"What are *you* doing here?" I asked Moose as he walked into the diner's kitchen a little before seven. It wasn't his usual habit of showing up near the end of our day.

"I came by to have a few words with you," he said. "I'm just glad that you're still open."

"Why wouldn't we be?" I asked. "It's not seven yet, is it?"

"No, but with the play tonight, I was afraid you might lock the doors early."

"There's not much chance of that happening," I said with a smile. "After all, I learned from the best, and someone once told me that unless there's an emergency of epic proportions, our doors stay open as long as the sign says they should be."

"That's my girl," Moose said with a grin. "Victoria, I think Jenny might need a little help cleaning up out front."

"I'm on it," I said. Jenny was our late afternoon and early evening waitress. During the day she took classes at the community college, and after she left us she normally pursued an extremely active social life, but she was a sweet girl, and a real asset to the diner.

I peeked my head out and saw that we were out of customers at the moment, and Jenny was sweeping the floor.

When she saw me, she said apologetically, "I hope you don't mind, but I got started on cleanup a little early since we didn't have any customers."

"I think it's brilliant," I said. "I'll be back to give you a hand in a second."

As I reentered the kitchen, I said, "Moose, there's nobody out there."

He'd been conferring with Greg at the grill, and as soon

as I walked in, my grandfather stopped talking instantly. "My mistake. Victoria, don't forget to come by my house after the show tonight. I expect an immediate update about what happened, okay?"

"We'll be there," I said.

"Good. Now, I need to get out of here. I can't keep your grandmother waiting all night."

After he was gone, I looked at Greg steadily as I asked, "What exactly was that all about just now?"

"I don't know what you're talking about," Greg said, refusing to make eye contact with me, a sure sign that he was holding something back.

"Greg, do you honestly believe that you can get away with that? How long have we been married, anyway?"

"That's a trick question," Greg said. "I told you before, I won't answer your marriage-related quiz questions anymore."

I laughed as I shook my head. "That's really nice."

"What's that?"

"The way you just tried to divert my suspicion. What did Moose tell you while I was in the dining room?"

Greg frowned. "I told him that I couldn't keep a secret from you."

I was intrigued now that my husband had even tried. "You were right. So give."

"He told me to keep an eye on you tonight, and if anything happened to you, I should get in my car and start driving, because if he ever caught up with me, that would be the end as far as I was concerned."

I was touched by my grandfather's concern, but not to the point where I'd easily forgive him saying something like that. "Greg, you have to forgive him. Sometimes Moose forgets that I'm a grown woman perfectly capable of taking care of myself."

"I don't see how he could *ever* forget that," Greg said.

"That's because you didn't help raise me. I'll have a word with him later. I can't have him threatening you like that, no matter what kind of motivation he thinks he has."

My husband looked extremely uncomfortable with the idea. "I'd really rather you didn't say anything to him at all, if it's all the same to you. I don't want him to think that I ran to you complaining, Victoria. I know that he's your grandfather, but he's my friend, and I don't want to disappoint him. Do you understand?"

"Completely. He expects the best out of us all, and it's hard to let him down, isn't it? Okay, I promise. I won't say a word."

"I appreciate that," Greg said. "Now, why don't you help Ellen so we can get out of here? It's going to be cutting it close if we don't hurry."

"Since when are you in such a rush to get to the theater?"

He grinned sheepishly. "I figure that the sooner we get there, the quicker we'll be able to leave."

"I hate to be the one to tell you, but your logic if flawed. It just doesn't work that way."

"Maybe so, but don't take away my last shred of hope, okay?"

"Okay," I said with a laugh. "Let's get cracking."

"Wow, it's déjà vu all over again," Greg said as we reentered the crowded theater lobby for the second night in a row. As he looked around the crowded room, he added, "I believe that Moose and Martha are the only ones who didn't come back for take two."

"They gave their tickets away to their neighbors, so it's no less crowded than it was before. Do you still have my cape with you?"

"It's right here," Greg said. "I still don't know why you brought it with you."

"It's backup for right now, but I might need it, so don't lose it."

"No, Ma'am," he said with a smile.

"Come on," I said as I tugged at his arm.

"Where are we going?"

"We're heading backstage before the play so we can do a little snooping. I have to thank you for that. We never would have had the time if you hadn't rushed me so much at home getting showered and changed."

"Remind me never to do that again," Greg said. "Victoria, you know that I'm not comfortable taking part in your investigations."

"You don't have to go with me if you don't want to, you know," I said as I stopped pulling his arm.

"Oh, no. I'm under strict orders that I'm not about to disobey. Wherever you go tonight, I go, too."

I wasn't sure how I felt about that. Sure, I loved the fact that Greg was concerned for my wellbeing, but then again, I wasn't all that crazy about having my husband follow me around while I tried to question some of my suspects.

When we got to the stage entrance off to one side, it looked as though it wasn't going to matter what I thought anyway.

There was a big, husky football player from the high school standing guard by the door, and from the looks of him, *no one* was going to get past.

Fortunately, the young man was a frequent patron of our diner, and I knew Peter Davis well. "Pete, I've never seen you in a suit before. How handsome you look."

He blushed a little from my praise. "You look nice too, Victoria." Almost as an afterthought, he looked at Greg and added, "Nice suit."

"Right back at you," my husband said.

"Peter, I was wondering if I could go backstage for one second before the show starts?" I asked.

The young man frowned. "I'm sorry, but I can't let you past me, Victoria. Mr. Wilkes is paying us all good money to keep these doors blocked, and he told me specifically that if anyone gets through from the auditorium, *none* of us will get paid. I'm really sorry about that."

"Don't worry," I said as I patted his arm. "I understand

completely."

"Are you sure?" he asked me. "Because I'd hate to have you mad at me."

"We're perfectly fine," I said. I leaned in a little closer and I asked him, "Do you know of any other ways in? I don't want you to lose your pay for the night, but this is important."

Peter looked around, and then he frowned. "Well, there might be one way that won't get me in trouble. If you use another entrance, Mr. Wilkes won't have any choice but to pay us. There's one door he forgot to post a guard on tonight. I almost said something, but then I realized that the information might come in handy, so I kept my mouth shut."

I looked at him carefully before I asked, "Peter, you're not asking me for a bribe, are you?"

He seemed honestly surprised by my suggestion. "Of course not. I just meant... what I meant to say was..."

Greg stepped in and saved him. "Don't take it personally; she does the same thing to me all the time. Victoria actually thinks it's funny to watch men squirm a little. The best thing you can do is just smile and pretend that she never asked you a question in the first place."

Peter nodded, and then he turned to me and offered his smile without uttering another word.

"I give up. Where's the door we need?" I asked with a smile after a few seconds of silence.

"I hope you're not spooked by it, but it's the outside door into Benny Booth's dressing room," Peter said. "I don't know if you know this about me, but I've always been interested in the theater."

"Do you want to be an actor?" I asked.

"No, what goes on behind the scenes is what interests me. I've even worked the spotlight on a few shows recently. That's kind of how I found out about the door being unlocked and all. I'm here so much that nobody even notices me when I go wandering around the building."

"Isn't Fred Hitchings using Benny's dressing room

tonight?" I asked.

"Nope. Evidently he was too spooked to get dressed there, so he's staying right where he was the night before. The room is empty right now; at least it was the last time I heard."

I nodded, and then I said, "Thanks so much. Come by the diner tomorrow, and I'll give you a free slice of pie." Peter was crazy about our pies, and he especially liked Greg's Crumb Apple.

"You've got yourself a deal," he said.

"Let's go, Greg," I said as I started toward the exit.

My husband asked, "Are we really going to sneak into a room where someone was murdered last night?"

"Do we have any choice?" I asked. "You're free to be my lookout if you'd like, but I'm going in there."

"Then I am, too," Greg said.

We walked outside and around the theater. The temperature was unseasonably chilly, and I was glad that I'd had Greg bring along my cape for more than just as a disguise. "Can I have my cape now, please?"

He handed it over, and I wrapped it around my shoulders, pulling the hood up over my hair in one easy motion.

"Now it's like being out with the Phantom of the Opera," Greg said as he checked out my new look.

"Laugh all you want, but this might come in handy, just you wait and see."

"I don't doubt it for one second," Greg said as we made our way around the building. There were several doors along the back of the building, but only one had a makeshift star stenciled on it. That had to be Benny Booth's door, and knowing the man even just a little, it wouldn't have surprised me one bit to learn that he'd most likely put that star there himself.

I tugged on the handle, but at first it resisted, and I wondered if someone had locked the dressing room door after Peter had spotted that it was unlocked.

It was just stuck a little, though. It released suddenly, and if Greg hadn't been standing there to put a hand on my back, there was no doubt in my mind that I would have taken a hard tumble, most likely ruining my fancy cape in the process.

"Thanks for that," I said.

"All part of the bodyguard service," he replied.

Taking a deep breath, I took one step forward into the room that had so recently seen a murder. I hadn't given it much thought until Peter had said something, but now I was downright spooked by the idea of going inside. Still, I'd spouted brave words before when I'd told the two men that I didn't mind doing it, so I had no other choice but to press ahead.

I could swear that there was a chill in the room that I could feel even through my cape as I walked across the threshold. "It's really cold in here, isn't it?"

"That's because they shut off the heat," Greg said. "Is it safe to flip on a light so I can open up a vent or two?"

"I'd really rather not. Besides, we won't be here that long. Let's press on." I pulled a small flashlight from my purse, and it came in handy once the dressing room door closed on its own behind us. "Let's get out of here as fast as we can."

"I can heartily go along with that," he said.

When I got to the door that led out into the hallway, I opened it slightly. There was a great deal of hustle and bustle going on backstage at the moment, and I didn't have a single doubt that I could slip in amongst them as though I belonged.

I wasn't so sure about my husband, though.

"Are you sure you want to go with me?" I asked Greg softly.

"I'm positive," he said.

As far as I could tell, no one was looking at the door to Benny's former dressing room at that moment, so I slipped through, with Greg close on my heels.

We were five steps inside when I heard Greg gasp behind

me.

"What are you doing back here, Greg?" It was the football coach himself, a man not unfamiliar with our diner fare at The Charming Moose. "It's supposed to be actors and crew only."

"Hey, Lou," I heard Greg say as I kept moving. I hated leaving my husband behind like that, but it didn't make sense to turn myself in, too, especially if the coach hadn't seen me. "Sorry about that. I must have gotten turned around."

"If you're looking for your wife, I haven't seen her back here," Lou said. "Is she in the play? I didn't see her name on any of the lists I got."

"No, we're both just here as theater lovers," Greg said. I came to a fold in a curtain and ducked into it, hoping to make anyone looking in my direction lose sight of me. The cape wasn't an exact match to the curtain material, but it wasn't that far off either, and besides, that fold offered pretty ample space.

"Well, you'd better take your seat. I'm sure that she's already there wondering where you wandered off to. Come on, let me give you a hand."

"Thanks, but I'm sure I can find it just fine on my own," Greg said.

"Me, too, but the boys and I are being paid pretty handsomely to keep folks out, and I don't want to be the one who lets them down. You understand, don't you?"

"Perfectly," he said. I risked one glance out of my safe haven and spotted Greg and Lou walking toward the exit together. I hated that we'd been separated, but at least now maybe I could do a little digging while Lou was otherwise occupied.

I headed for the next dressing room in line and saw that someone had written Sandra Hall's name on a piece of tape and had stuck it there. Fame was fleeting, there was no doubt about that. On either side of her door were photos of past actors and actresses all holding their wing-handled Jaspers, and I wondered how they must feel having them displayed so prominently like that. They were proud most likely, even though the award was little known outside of the Jasper Fork Community Theater Circuit.

Taking a chance, I knocked on the door, and after a moment's delay, I heard a woman inside say, "Enter," so I did.

It was time to interview one of our main suspects, and I hoped that there was a chance I'd be able to catch her off-guard. Otherwise, I might soon find myself ejected as well, and I didn't know how I was going to begin to explain that to Moose later that night.

As I stepped inside, I said, "Five minutes," though I had no idea if that were true or not. It was an excuse to get in, and I hoped that it would be accurate enough.

"Very good," Sandra Hall said with smug approval. She was a pretty woman; I could see that even under the overstated makeup she was wearing now, and unless I missed my guess, she had a figure to match, though that was disguised as well under a frumpy and faded frock that had seen better days, say in the seventies. "I'm glad to see that I wasn't forgotten this time. Where were you last night? If I hadn't stumbled out on my own, I would have missed my first cue."

"I didn't make it in last night," I said. "It's a shame about your leading man, isn't it?"

"The man was a baked ham if ever there was one," Sandra said. "Not that Fred Hitchings is going to be any better. I don't know why I let Garret Wilkes talk me into this."

"So, you and Benny didn't get along?" I asked.

"I just said that, didn't I? Now, isn't there someone else you need to go bother? I'm preparing for my role."

"I'm sure you are. Did you and Benny prepare together last night before the play, maybe in his dressing room?"

"What kind of question is that? Of course not. I never stepped one toe into his dressing room, and I wouldn't allow him in mine, either. Booth claimed to be a method actor, though I'm sure he wouldn't know what that meant if Strasberg himself explained it to him."

I had no idea who or what a Strasberg was, but I decided to keep that to myself. Instead, I laughed knowingly, and Sandra nodded her head slightly with approval.

"When was the last time you *did* see him?" I asked.

"Hours before the show yesterday. Garret Wilkes demanded that we all meet one last time, and there was no way to get out of it, so I showed up, albeit reluctantly." Sandra frowned for a second, and then she asked me, "Who are you, exactly?"

"Me? I'm nobody; just another wannabe," I said, hoping she'd let it go at that.

She wouldn't. "I know you. You're Victoria from The Charming Moose, aren't you?"

Okay, it wasn't a major disaster that she recognized me. After all, I hadn't asked her anything that outlandish. "That's just what I do to put bread on the table. What I live for is acting." Wow, it sounded like a load of garbage even as I said it, but Sandra seemed to buy it.

"Oh, I understand."

I would have been fine if the real stagehand had forgotten to alert Sandra again, but to my dismay, there was a tap at the door, and it opened to show a brawny young man with a brand new haircut standing there. "Five minutes, Ms. Hall," the man said, and then he frowned when he noticed that I was there, too.

"Yes, yes, I already heard."

"How's that possible?" the man asked. "That's *my* job tonight."

"Yesterday no one informed me of the time, and tonight, two people do. What kind of production is this, anyway?" She raised her voice as she said the last bit of it. I just hoped that it wouldn't attract any undue attention.

Again, my hopes were thwarted.

Garret Wilkes, the producer/director himself, popped his head in through the door. "What seems to be the problem here?"

I tried to hide behind my cape, but of course it didn't work. He recognized me immediately. "Victoria, what are you doing here?"

"I was invited," I said, hoping that Sandra wouldn't rat me out. After all, for all she knew, I could have been.

Just not by her.

"Be that as it may, I need to ask you to leave. How did you get in?"

"I waited around in back for someone to show up and let me in. I got tired of waiting though, so I tried the door myself. It was unlocked, so I just walked on in."

He frowned at my story, but at least I'd saved Peter and his friends their pay. "Junior, please escort this woman back to her seat." Garret studied my cape for a moment, and then he asked, "You do have a seat, don't you?"

"Oh, yes," I said. "I wouldn't miss this for the world." I was about to wish Sandra Hall good luck, but then I remembered that was considered bad form in the theater. "Break a leg," I told her instead, finding it odd to wish that on anyone.

I was sent back to my seat, and Greg was grinning at me when I arrived with a husky young escort.

"So, they got you too, did they? Thanks for abandoning me like that," my husband said with a broad grin. "Were you able to find anything out?"

The lights started to dim, so I said, "Later," and turned my attention to the play.

After ninety minutes, I was ready to go home, soak in a hot tub, and try to forget every last bit of the debacle I'd just seen. Fred Hitchings had muffed just about every line he had, and that had thrown Sandra's timing off as well. She might have been fairly good given the right supporting cast, but as it was, instead of elevating everyone else's performance, she managed to be dragged down to their level kicking and screaming.

As the crowd offered its tepid applause at the end of the play, Greg said, "Well, I'll never get those six hours of my life back."

"What are you talking about? It was just an hour and a half long," I said.

"You're kidding. It felt like *days*."

"Well, it wasn't," I said with a smile. "Let's go talk to Moose and then head home. I need a good long soak tonight."

"Sure, but you're going to tell *me* what you found out first, aren't you? After all, I'm the one who had to sit through that mess."

"Okay, but you're just getting the highlights."

"I can live with that," he said.

There wasn't much to tell, but I shared what I'd learned, and Greg seemed satisfied enough with it.

I just hated to tell Moose how little I'd learned, but it couldn't be helped.

We shared everything, no matter how small, and this was about the least I'd ever gotten on my own.

Chapter 8

"Come on in. We've been waiting forever for you,"
Moose told us as we walked into his house.

"If you think *that* was forever, you should have seen the
play," Greg said. "Hi, Martha. How are you?"

"I'm fine. Do you have any interest joining me in the
kitchen while these two compare notes? You're most
welcome, unless you'd rather stay in the living room with
them."

"Not on your life," Greg said. "Lead the way."

Martha smiled, and then she turned to Moose and me.
"There's a pie that's due out of the oven in eleven minutes,
so if you can wrap up your discussion by then, you're
welcome to join us in the kitchen."

"If we take fifteen minutes, will you still wait for us?"
Moose asked his wife with a grin.

"Not even if it's just thirteen," Martha said as she and
Greg retreated into the kitchen. I knew that neither of them
was a big fan of our investigations, though they admitted the
necessity of them. Still, they were both in our corner, and
my grandfather and I knew that we could count on our
spouses whenever we needed them.

"Talk to me," Moose said.

I gave him a recap of what I'd seen and heard,
emphasizing Sandra Hall's claim that she had never even
been in Benny's dressing room, let alone kill him. "If we can
trip her up there, we've got her," Moose said.

"How are we going to do that?"

"All we need to do is find one person who saw Sandra
Hall in Benny's dressing room, whether it was the night of
the murder or not, and we've caught her in a lie. Wouldn't
you say that would indicate that she's our killer?"

I hated that phrase, 'our killer,' but I didn't say anything to Moose. "Not necessarily. What if she was lying about being there to cover something else up?"

"Victoria, what's worse than being accused of murder?" Moose asked.

"In Sandra's mind, admitting to having an affair with the man might just be worse."

My grandfather's eyebrow raised. "Are you holding out any new information from me, Victoria?"

"No, I'm just repeating some of the rumors that I've heard. Benny could be charming when it suited his purpose, even you have to admit that."

"I'll admit nothing of the sort," Moose said curtly. "The man was never charming to me in all the years I knew him."

"That's either because he couldn't fool you, or he never wanted anything from you," I replied.

"Did you have any luck with any of the rest of the cast?"

"I never really got a chance to question anyone else," I admitted. "Besides, I've now spoken with our entire list of suspects."

"So far, then, we have Sandra Hall, Fred Hitchings, Marcus Jackson, Vern Jeffries, Garret Wilkes, and Amanda Lark. That's pretty impressive, isn't it?"

"I don't mind adding any more names to the roster if we have a reason for it, but as things stand, I believe that we very well could have the killer listed among those names."

Moose nodded. "I agree. The real question is what do we do about it?"

I glanced at the clock on the wall. "Well, it's too late to do any more interviews tonight. I think we should wait until morning and get a fresh start. Do you think Martha would mind coming into the diner and covering for me after my eight a.m. shift?"

"I'm sure that she'd be delighted. Would you like me to ask her for you?"

"No, I don't mind doing it myself."

We were still talking about the possibilities when Martha

poked her head into the living room. "This is your first and last warning. Pie is now being served in the kitchen, and if you're nice, there might just be a scoop of ice cream to go along with it."

Moose stood quickly, and I followed suit. "You don't have to tell us twice," Moose said with a grin.

"I wasn't about to," she said, smiling brightly.

More than an hour later, we were saying our good nights. Despite my early shift the next morning, I'd been the one to prolong our visit. While it was true that we saw plenty of my grandparents at the diner, the opportunity to spend time with them both when we were away from the place was a little too rare for my taste.

As we pulled into our driveway back at home, I said, "That was great, Greg. I'm so lucky that I still have my grandparents so close by."

"I couldn't imagine a world without them in it," Greg agreed. As we got out of the car, I pulled my jacket close. The day had been quite nice, but it had turned chilly with the setting sun, and a cold breeze was blowing.

I glanced at the darkened front door, and I was glad that Greg had installed a motion detector on the light over it a few months earlier. When we got within twenty feet of it in the dark, it would spring to life. I looked forward to it turning itself on when I saw something moving!

"Greg, hold on a second," I said as I grabbed his arm.

"What is it, Victoria?" he asked. "I'm not in the mood to dawdle. I should have worn a heavier jacket."

"Something's near the front door," I said. "See?"

As I said it, there was movement again. It wasn't a person, or even an animal; I could see that now. It looked like something flapping in the breeze. But what could it be?

"There's no sense standing around trying to figure out what it is. Let's go see for ourselves," Greg said as he took another step forward, and the light sprang into its full intensity.

"It's just a note," I said as relief flooded through me. Sure enough, someone had left a message for us, but they'd chosen a rather unconventional way of delivering it.

A sheet ripped from a small notebook was pinned to the wood of the door jamb with an ice pick, its shaft dripping in blood.

At least that was what it had looked like at first.

"It's not blood after all," I said after I gave it a closer look, feeling relieved and clearly showing it in my voice. "It's just paint."

"Maybe so, but it's still a pretty nasty way to deliver a message," Greg said as he reached to pull the ice pick out of the door frame.

"Hang on. The sheriff needs to see this," I said as I grabbed his arm and stopped him.

"Why should he possibly care about somebody's idea of a bad joke? What does it mean, BACK OFF? You think this is related to the murder, don't you?"

"How could it not be?" I asked. "It's pretty clear that somebody's trying to warn us that we're getting too close."

"Victoria, if that's true, how can you sound so pleased when you say that?" Greg asked as he pulled out his cell phone.

"At least it means that we're onto something," I said. "Let me call Sheriff Croft."

"Fine. If you need me, I'll be inside warming up." Greg put away his phone, stared off into the gloom outside the light's reach, and then he asked, "You don't suppose whoever did this is still out there, do you?"

"Don't worry, they are bound to be long gone. After all, why deliver a warning and then stick around to see that we get it? If they'd wanted to hurt me, they wouldn't have alerted me first, now would they?"

"Maybe so, but I'm staying right here with you until the police show up," Greg said.

"I thought you were cold."

"What do you know? I suddenly warmed up," he said, and I knew that I couldn't dissuade him from staying with me.

"Sheriff, it's Victoria. Do you have a second?"

"I've got a quite few. One of my deputies is off tonight, and I'm filling in for her. What can I do for you?"

"I just thought you might like to see this. Somebody used what looks like a bloody ice pick to pin a warning onto my door."

"Where are you, at the café?" The casual nature of our conversation was gone in an instant.

"No, Greg and I are at home. Should I take it down, or would you like to see it for yourself first?"

"Don't touch a thing, I'll be there in a few minutes."

After he hung up, I turned to Greg. "He's on his way over."

"I've got an idea. Why don't we wait for him inside?" Greg asked.

"Okay, but I need to do something first."

"You're not taking that note down after warning me not to, are you?"

"No, but I'm going to get a few pictures of it while I still can," I said. "Who knows? It might come in handy later."

"Should I get your camera?" Greg asked as he started for the door.

"Yes, but I'll go ahead and get started with the camera on my phone." My husband hesitated at the door, and I added, "It's on the kitchen counter. You won't be gone thirty seconds."

"Don't do anything crazy while I'm gone."

"Even I can't get in trouble that fast," I said.

Greg was back in twenty seconds though, just in case.

I'd managed to get four good shots with my phone in the meantime, so I switched over to my real camera when he came back out. "How'd you manage to grab a jacket, too? You didn't have enough time."

"It was on the couch. I meant to wear it today, but I

changed my mind at the last second." He shuddered a little. "That really is a nasty little note, isn't it?"

"It doesn't really surprise me. Whoever did it clearly has a fondness for the dramatic, wouldn't you say? After all, it's not something just anyone would think to do."

"So, do you think that it's somebody from the play?"

"Either that," I said, "or someone is trying to make it look that way."

"Then, it doesn't really do you much good, does it?"

I finished taking one more shot as I saw headlights heading toward us. Unless I missed my guess, that would be the sheriff. I took one last photograph, and then I tucked my camera into my pocket. There was no use advertising the fact that I'd fully documented the threat before the sheriff showed up to do his own investigation.

He got out of the cruiser and walked toward us with real purpose. "I don't suppose you saw who did this, did you?"

"We were at Moose and Martha's place," I said, deciding not to mention that we'd been at the theater before that.

The sheriff nodded, and then he took a few photographs of his own, though not nearly as many as I had. He talked softly as he worked, whether to us or to himself, I wasn't sure. "Just paint," he said, and then he added, "Block letters, and the paper's common enough, too."

After Sheriff Croft was satisfied with the record, he donned a pair of gloves and carefully removed the ice pick, working it free and catching the note as soon as it was clear. The pick went into one evidence bag, while the note went into another.

When he had everything stowed carefully away, the sheriff turned to me. "Now, just who have you been antagonizing in the twenty-four hours since Benny got himself killed?"

"It's been twenty-eight, actually," I said as I glanced at my watch, "and the list is too long to go over out here. Why don't you come inside and I'll make us all a pot of coffee?"

"Better yet, I'll make it while the two of you have

yourselves a little chat," Greg said.

The sheriff nodded. "That sounds good. You wouldn't happen to have any pie around, would you?"

My husband smiled. "Sheriff, if there's not pie in my house, then I'm not living here. How does Dutch apple sound to you?"

"Like a real treat on a chilly evening," he said, the pleasure coming through clear in his voice. "What say we go on in and get started, Victoria?"

"I'm game if you are, but I hope you're going to share a little with me, too, when I'm finished telling all that I know."

"I might, but I'm not making any promises."

"Then we'll give you coffee, but I can't guarantee that you'll get any pie," I said.

"Don't pay any attention to her. She can't threaten you with that," Greg said. "I made that pie myself, and I'll share it with anyone I care to."

I grinned at the sheriff. "Okay, you caught me. I was bluffing. You can have some pie, whether you tell my anything or not."

Greg patted my shoulder and smiled as he walked into the kitchen to start the coffee. "Now, where should I begin?"

"Knowing you, you've got a list of suspects around here somewhere."

"As a matter of fact, I do. Should I text it to your phone?"

The sheriff shook his head. "Let's do this the old-fashioned way. You talk, I'll listen and take notes, and if I need you to elaborate on anything, I'll ask a few questions."

"Have it your way," I said, "but I'm still going to refer to my list."

"Be my guest," he said as he settled in on the couch.

I called up the picture of our whiteboard on my phone, and then I got started.

"Mostly, we've just got the obvious," I said. "I'm sure you've already looked at the people on our list yourself."

"Indulge me," he said.

"Fred Hitchings is first up. He wanted that lead bad enough to taste it."

"Do you think that he'd actually kill Benny to get a role?" the sheriff asked.

"You should talk to him about it and hear him," I said. "The man's a little crazy when it comes to acting. Are you going to let me get through this, or are you going to quiz me on every motive I give you?"

"I'll try to restrain myself until you're finished," he said with a wry grin.

"Sandra Hall is next. We believe she might have had a brief fling with Benny that went bad fast. Next is her boyfriend, Marcus Jackson. He's a personal trainer and the man has a very bad temper. Garret Wilkes, the director, had some real issues with Benny on and off the stage. Benny was dating Amanda Lark before he dumped her recently, and she took it harder than she's letting on, and finally, we have Vern Jeffries, Benny's former business partner. There are rumors all over town that Benny cheated him out of a great deal of money, and Moose and I both figure he's a good candidate to be the killer."

"You're logic is sound, but you can cross his name off your list," the sheriff said. "Vern didn't do it."

I couldn't believe the sheriff was telling me that. Vern had been high on our list, and his alibi had been nonexistent. "How can you say that? He has no alibi. The man told Moose and me that he was in his office sitting at his desk working alone all night."

"That's right. One of my officers was driving past on his rounds during the time of the murder, and Vern was there both times my officer looked in. There's no way he had time to get to the theater, kill Benny, and get back to his desk in time."

"How sure are you of that as an alibi?" I asked, reluctant to give up such a good suspect.

"As sure as I need to be."

"Okay, thanks for sharing that," I said. "Any other tidbits

you might have for us?"

"Well, I have photos from the crime scene, but I'm not sure you'll want to see them," the sheriff said. "Some of them are pretty graphic."

"I'll take a quick peek, if you don't mind," I said as I steeled myself for what I was about to see. The photos of Benny I quickly passed over, as well as the bloody trophy that had been used to kill him. There was blood encrusted on the engravings, as well as on the elegantly plain handles. Someone must have really walloped him with that thing. I suddenly couldn't take it anymore, and I pushed the photos back to the sheriff.

"Thanks. Is there anything else I should know about?"

"No, that's about it. Victoria, you've done fairly well on your own. You and Moose have been quite thorough."

"But what about the note?" I asked.

"I have a hunch that you're not far off. *Wherever* it came from, it's not good."

"Do you agree with me, then? That note *has* to mean that Moose and I have already talked to whoever killed Benny. Why else would anyone leave me such an over-the-top warning?"

"Chances are you are right, but that's still a mighty big list of suspects you've got. You have to watch your back all of the time if you're going to pursue this." He closed up his notebook and stood. "Tell your husband that I had to leave," the sheriff said.

"You're not staying for pie?"

"Thanks, but I'd better not," he said.

"Greg won't be happy about that," I said.

"Happy about what?" my husband asked as he walked into the living room.

"I'm sorry, but I can't stay," the sheriff said.

Greg frowned broadly. "Are you telling me that this town can't live without you for five minutes? Come on, Sheriff, I won't take no for an answer."

My husband could be pretty persuasive when he wanted

to, but I could see that the sheriff was still uncertain.

I decided that it was time that I spoke up. "No more talk about the murder investigation if you stay. I promise."

He looked at me closely, and then the sheriff said, "Okay, if you're sure you have enough pie to spare."

"Sheriff, that's the great thing about pie. If we run out, I can always make more," Greg said with a grin.

"Okay, then. Thank you."

The three of us spent a pleasant fifteen minutes over pie and coffee, and I found myself enjoying the sheriff's company. When we weren't clashing over a murder investigation, he could be a pretty good guy. After he told us a funny story about arresting the same woman for speeding three times in the same night, he stood and stretched. "Greg, that pie was so good, it should be illegal."

"I hope it never is," I said, "because I love it, too."

My husband smiled. "I appreciate the fact that you both enjoyed it so much."

As Sheriff Croft was leaving, he said, "Be careful, Victoria."

"Do you mean that you aren't even going to ask her to stop?" Greg asked him with a grin.

The sheriff turned to me as he asked, "Would it do any good?"

"What do you think?" I asked, smiling broadly.

"That's why I asked you to be careful. Let me know if anything else happens. And remember, it doesn't have to be this dramatic. If anything out of the ordinary happens, I want to hear about it, okay?"

"Okay," I said.

After the police cruiser was gone, I said, "He's really not such a bad guy, is he?"

"You both want the same thing," Greg said. "You just go about it differently."

"All I really care about is that one of us finds out who killed Benny. It doesn't matter to me if he does it, or Moose and I do. I hate the stories that are spreading around town about my grandparents."

"Don't worry, you'll crack this case. I know it."

"I wish I had *your* confidence in me," I said.

"You don't need it, Victoria. I've got enough for both of us."

Later, after Greg was asleep, rest still eluded me. Moose and I had obviously gotten to someone, but who? I would have been a lot happier if I had a single clue that definitively pointed to who killed Benny, but for now, all I had were a handful of educated guesses.

Hopefully tomorrow would bring something a little more concrete.

Oh, no. I'd forgotten to call Moose after Greg and I had found the note pinned to the door! I thought about waiting until tomorrow, but if he got wind of what happened before I could tell him, I'd never hear the end of it.

I got out of bed, slipped on my robe, grabbed my phone, and then I tiptoed downstairs.

Chapter 9

"Did I wake you?" I asked Moose as he picked up on the second ring. There was a sleepiness in his voice that I instantly recognized, and I suddenly regretted calling him so late.

"No, I'm mostly still awake. I've been reading the latest Gresham novel, and I can't put it down. I had fun tonight, Victoria."

"So did I," I said. "Something happened when Greg and I got home, though."

The softness left his voice immediately. "What happened?"

"Someone took an ice pick, dipped it in red paint, and then they stuck it into our door jamb," I said. "There was a note pinned to the wood that said, BACK OFF."

"So, we got to somebody today," Moose said, clearly pleased. He must have realized that the tone in his voice wasn't entirely appropriate. "I didn't mean to sound so pleased that you were threatened tonight, Victoria; you know that, don't you?"

"Don't worry about it. I had the exact same reaction, though Greg and the sheriff weren't nearly as pleased by it."

"You called the sheriff?" Moose asked.

"Yes. Why? Don't you think I should have?"

"Of course, it was the right thing to do. I suppose he wanted to know what we've been up to. Did you tell him?"

"Every fact, suspicion, and supposition," I said. "That's our policy, remember? Never hold anything back from the police."

"Yes, I stand by it, too. You did the right thing. What did he have to say?"

"He told me that we were doing a good job, and he also let me know that we could drop Vern Jeffries from our list of suspects. One of his deputies spotted him at his desk twice within a short amount of time when Benny was murdered. The sheriff was pretty certain that Vern couldn't have done it."

"Then we'll strike him from our list," Moose said. "That still leaves us with quite a few suspects. Did he offer any other insights?"

"He told me to be careful, but he didn't tell me to stop digging," I said.

"I'm sure he realized that it would have been useless. So, where does this leave us?"

"If you're up for it, we should push even harder tomorrow. With Martha filling in for me at the diner, we can start pestering people as soon as you get there."

"Sorry, but it's going to have to be after eleven."

"Why not bright and early?" I asked.

"I have a doctor's appointment," Moose said.

I suddenly felt an icy fist grab my heart. "What's wrong?"

He read my tone of voice beautifully. "Nothing, child. Don't worry about me. At my age, going to the doctor is routine."

"You're not lying to me, are you?" I asked. I couldn't imagine my world without my grandfather in it.

"No, that's something I wouldn't dream of ever doing. Now, we both need to hang up and get some sleep. Your grandmother and I will be at the diner tomorrow by eleven, and you and I can get busy figuring out who murdered Benny Booth. I don't know why, but I thought it would be easier than it's turning out to be."

"Why would you think that? The man seemed to collect enemies like some folks collect stamps or coins."

"I don't know. I just thought that one of our candidates would be more obvious than we've found them to be."

"Who knows? Maybe we'll have better luck tomorrow," I said.

"Maybe so. I'd really like to uncover who did it before

they escalate beyond threatening notes."

"I agree," I said.

I had no trouble falling asleep after that. I'd done all that I could, at least for tonight.

Let tomorrow's troubles stay right where they were.

For now, I needed my sleep.

"Is there something wrong with your eggs?" I asked Martin Race the next the morning as he had breakfast at the diner. Martin always had three eggs, over medium, bacon that was barely cooked, and toast that was dry enough to use as sandpaper. It was something that had been his regular meal for the past six years, and he didn't even have to order it anymore. All it took was a wave, a smile, and the single word, 'Usual,' and we were set.

Apparently not today, though.

He moved the eggs around on his plate, and it was pretty clear that he hadn't taken a single bite. "I'm really sorry, but these just won't do."

"I can't see anything wrong with them, but if you'd like fresh ones, I'll get Mom to make them for you. They'll be ready in a jiff," I said as I whisked the plate away.

"It won't help," he said sullenly.

"What will, then?" I asked.

"I'm just sick of eggs, that's all," Martin said with a sigh. "Victoria, I'll be happy to pay for this, but I just can't choke down a single bite of it today."

It would take more than that to throw me off balance. "Well, we have lots of other choices. Would you like to see a menu?"

"I left my reading glasses at home. Would you mind telling me yourself?"

The place wasn't crowded, so I indulged him. "Let's see. We've got French toast, pancakes, waffles, breakfast burritos, and oatmeal. Do any of those choices grab you?"

"No, I'm afraid not."

"I'm not ready to give up yet. If you'd like a hamburger

or a grilled cheese sandwich and some soup, I'm sure Mom could rustle something up for you in the kitchen."

"Nope, none of that sounds good, either." His frown vanished as he asked, "How about pie?"

"We've got plenty of that. There's apple, peach, pecan, and chocolate on the menu today."

"I'll have apple," he said.

"One slice coming up," I replied.

"No, you misunderstood me. I want the whole pie, and I'll eat it right here."

"Would you like some ice cream with it?" I asked, having a hard time believing that anyone could eat an entire pie for breakfast.

"No, I'll eat it plain. Oh, and bring me a tall glass of milk, too."

"I'm on it," I said.

I brought the plate of eggs into the kitchen and scraped it into the trash. Of course Mom noticed. "Was there something wrong with Martin's breakfast?"

"No. He just suddenly had his fill of eggs."

Mom rubbed her hands together. "I can make him anything he'd like."

"You don't have to," I said with a smile. "All he wants is apple pie."

"Pie? For breakfast?"

"What can I say? He's a man. Greg's done it before, and it wouldn't surprise me if Dad and Moose haven't been tempted before themselves."

"What is it with men and pie?" she asked as she got one out of the case and started to cut it.

"Hang on. I said that he wanted a pie, not a slice."

"He's going to eat the entire thing?" she asked in wonder.

"I'm not sure if he's going to make it, but that's his intention."

"Good enough," Mom said as she handed me the whole pie.

I delivered it, and as I slid the apple pie in front of him, I asked Martin, "Would you like me to cut you a piece of it to start?"

"Thanks, but I've always wanted to dig into an entire pie all by myself."

"Here's a fork, then. Bon appetite."

Martin looked at the pie with great affection before he stuck his fork into it, and I marveled as he started his assault with only a fork and a hungry expression on his face.

I was still watching him with wonder ten minutes later when the front door opened. I was hoping for another customer, but this was even better.

One of our suspects was coming into the diner, and if I played it right, it might just save Moose and me a trip later.

Marcus Jackson approached the register where I stood. "We need to talk."

"I thought that was what we were doing," I said.

"It's about Benny and Sandra," he said curtly.

"By all means, then. Is there something you want to tell me about them?"

He looked around the diner, and though our crowd was sparse at the moment, I knew that could change any second.

"Could we chat over there?"

"As long as no one needs me, I'm all yours," I said. As we walked to a nearby table away from everyone else, I asked, "Would you like some coffee?"

"Caffeine is poison to your body," he said.

"Maybe to yours, but that's all I run on most days," I said. I had planned to get us both cups, but after that, I figured that I could skip a coffee break just this once. "So, what about Benny and Sandra?"

"I knew what was going on between them," Marcus said. "It wasn't like it was unexpected, you know? I've learned to live with it."

"Has Sandra been unfaithful to you before?" I asked. It was hard to believe that this overblown physique of a man wouldn't have a problem with his girlfriend cheating on him.

"Every play she's ever been in," Marcus said glumly. "I didn't like it, but I can't say that she didn't warn me when we first started going out. She said it was the only way she could get into character, and that if I couldn't understand that about her, then we didn't belong together."

"That must be brutal for you," I said, suddenly feeling a little sympathy for Marcus. "Is that why you pitched such a fit at the theater during rehearsal?" I couldn't imagine anyone putting up with such nonsense, but from the pain I saw in his eyes, I realized that the man might not have had much choice in the matter, at least not in his mind.

"I can live with it most of the time, but all of a sudden, it hit me hard," he said. "But I got over it. I didn't really have much choice, not if I want to stay with Sandra."

"How many plays has she been in since you've been together?"

"Three," Marcus said glumly. "I'll admit that Benny was the worst for me, but I wouldn't kill him for what he did. When it came down to it, I couldn't even blame the poor sap. There aren't many men who could resist Sandra if she threw herself at them."

"I don't know how you do it," I said. "I know that I couldn't."

"It all boils down to the fact that I'd rather have a part of her affection than none of it. I guess it's some kind of addiction."

"That's the only way that I can even begin to understand it," I said. "Marcus, I don't really know you at all, but don't you deserve better than that?"

"I don't know anymore," he said. "I didn't mean to get into all of this with you. I just wanted you and your grandfather to know the truth. Sandra and I are both innocent."

"But you can't really know that, can you?" I asked him.

"I know it in my heart. Can I prove it? No. But it's true just the same."

"Were you *really* in her dressing room the entire time

when Benny was killed?" I asked him.

"I wasn't lying to you when I told you that. Every word I said to you the last time that we talked was true. I didn't kill that man, and neither did Sandra."

"You didn't happen to leave me a note last night, did you?" I asked as I watched his eyes.

"I don't have a clue what you're talking about," he said. I'd watched his face, and unless he was a better actor than his girlfriend, he was most likely telling me the truth. Then again, I had no way to judge just how good an actor he might be.

Marcus stood, and I marveled again at how strong the man looked. I doubted that he'd need a trophy to kill Benny if he put his mind to it.

I stood as well. "Thanks for coming by."

"Does that mean that you'll leave Sandra alone? She'd be embarrassed to know that I told you all that I did this morning."

Wow. Sleeping with her costars didn't embarrass her, but other folks finding out about her indiscretions did? "I'll do what I can, but I can't make any promises," I said.

Marcus's face clouded up, and I could feel his presence even stronger. "I wouldn't like it if you keep bothering her, Victoria."

"I'm sorry, but I can't do anything about that. We have to go where our investigation leads us, and right now, Sandra stays on our list of suspects."

"I don't understand it," Marcus said as he scowled. "Why did I waste my time coming here, if you're not going to do what I ask?"

"At least you got it off your chest."

He got really close, and then Marcus said softly, "Don't make me mad, Victoria. You won't like it when I'm angry, I promise you that."

I felt chills race up and down my spine. This was a real threat, one so intense that it shook me.

This wasn't a cowardly note left pinned to my door jamb.

This was a direct confrontation.

"What's going on here?" I heard Moose ask as he walked over to us. He'd just come from the kitchen, but I hadn't even seen him come into the diner.

"We were just chatting," I said, trying to ignore Marcus's threat.

"That's not what it looked like to me," Moose said as he got in the big man's face. "Is there a problem here?"

"No problem, Gramps," he said as he tried to shove Moose aside. Marcus was clearly surprised when my grandfather held his ground. Moose might not have been as muscle-bound as Marcus was, but he was solid, and all those years of standing behind the grill had given him the ability to plant himself like a tree if he didn't want to be moved.

Moose didn't answer; he just stood there staring right back at Marcus.

"Whatever," the personal trainer said as he sidestepped Moose and walked out of the diner without another word.

"What was that about?" Moose asked as soon as Marcus was gone.

I looked around and saw that we were attracting an audience. Even Martin was watching us closely, despite doing his best to demolish that apple pie singlehandedly.

"I thought you had a doctor's appointment this morning," I asked.

"I cancelled it. That can wait. This can't."

"Are you sure about that?" I asked him.

"Stop worrying about me, Victoria. I'm fine."

I was going to have to take his word for it. "Is Martha with you?"

"She's in the kitchen talking to your mother. Why?"

"I'd just rather not get into it right here right now," I said. "It can wait until we're in the truck. We're still digging into Benny's murder, aren't we?"

"You bet we are," he said. "Let me just tell them we're going, and we'll be on our way. Would you like to wait for me in the truck?"

"Sure, why not?" I asked. I walked outside, got into the passenger side of Moose's truck, and then I waited for him. I wish I hadn't looked around to see if Marcus were somewhere nearby, but if I said that I didn't, I'd be lying. It was with more than a hint of relief for me when Moose walked out and got in on the driver's side.

"I'm not starting this thing until you tell me what happened," Moose said.

After I brought him up to date on what Marcus had told me, my grandfather asked, "Do you believe him?"

"Which part, the threat, or what he said about his relationship with Sandra Hall?"

"Both, I guess."

"Yes and no," I said. "Marcus may believe that he's okay with Sandra's behavior, but I doubt that he is. It killed him to tell me about it, and the only reason he did was to get us to leave his girlfriend alone."

"How about the threat he made?" Moose asked.

"Oh yes, I had no trouble believing that was real. We need to talk to her first thing."

"You're not afraid of Marcus?" my grandfather asked.

"Of course I am. I'm not an idiot. But think about it. There's a good chance that Marcus isn't working right now if he had time to come by the diner. That means that if Sandra is at the gym, he's probably not going to be around to interfere."

"You're intrepid, if nothing else," Moose told me.

"Thanks. I think," I said.

"There's nothing wrong with being brave, Victoria," he said. "Just be sure that you can deal with the consequences."

"I'm as sure as I'll ever be," I said.

"Good enough. Let's go see Sandra, then."

"I just hope she's in."

Chapter 10

We got lucky with our investigation, which happens every now and then, but not nearly enough, at least in my opinion. Sandra was working at the gym despite what Marcus had told us the day before, and what's more, she was just finishing up with a customer when Moose and I walked in.

"I wanted to come by and apologize for the mix-up in your dressing room last night. You were wonderful last night," I said.

"Really," she said calmly. "I appreciate your kind words, but I'm not so sure that I was. I thought *Benny* was a hack, but he looked like Olivier compared to Fred Hitchings."

"Aren't you two close now that you're acting together?" I asked. I wanted to see if what Marcus had told us was true. If it was, it meant that Sandra was already having a fling with her new costar.

"No," she said, the disgust evident on her face. "I'm afraid that he's ruined some of my most valuable acting techniques for me forever."

I had to wonder if that meant that she was no longer getting intimate with her costars, but for the life of me, I couldn't find a way to ask her without embarrassing myself.

Moose clearly had no such compunction. "Does that mean that you're not favoring him with any *special* attention?"

"What do you mean by that?" she asked, daring him to elaborate.

That was a dangerous road she was about to embark on, knowing my grandfather as I did. It was time to step in before he had a chance to answer the question. "It's not important. We understand that you were in the restroom when Benny was killed. Did you have a touch of food poisoning?"

"No, I won't pretend that my nerves weren't on edge, especially since it was clear from the beginning that it was going to be up to me to carry the play. It's not at all unusual for great actors to have nerves before a performance, especially opening night."

"Was anyone there with you the entire time?" I asked her.

"No, other actresses were in and out, and it wouldn't surprise me if half of them didn't even know that I was there. I kept to myself, and I didn't invite anyone's sympathy or understanding. I do what I must do. Why are you really here, Victoria? Are you interested in a membership?"

"Not as interested as we are in asking you some questions," I said.

Sandra frowned. "Marcus warned me that you might be by, but he told me not ten minutes ago that he'd dealt with you both once and for all."

"I'm afraid that might have been wishful thinking on his part," I said. "He told me about your arrangement, but I can't believe that he wasn't more jealous than he was."

"Jealousy is for the commoners," she said almost regally. "Marcus understands my process, and he accepts me as I am."

"You shouldn't treat him like he's disposable," I said, letting my personal feelings interfere with our investigation for a second. I wasn't a big fan of Marcus by any means, but that didn't mean that I thought he deserved the bad treatment he was getting. "People deserve better than that."

She laughed at my statement. "My, I never dreamed that Marcus could count on you as one of his defenders. It is what it is, and he knows that he's free to look for someone else whenever he pleases. I can't change my ways."

"Can't, or won't?" Moose asked.

"I'm bored with this. If you're not interested in starting a membership, I have work to do."

"One more thing," I said. "You didn't happen to be the

one who left a note at my house last night, were you? If you did, you forgot to sign it."

"I have nothing to say to you in person, so why would I ever leave you a note? Now, you both need to leave."

I put on my brightest plastic smile. "Sandra, that's no way to treat a potential customer, is it? I'm sure your manager would be pleased to get my input about your attitude, unless you're *acting* with him, too." I knew that I shouldn't have said it the second the words left my lips, but I hadn't been able to help myself.

She stared at me icily as she said, "What I do with whom I choose is no one's business but mine. If you're looking for who killed Benny, you're talking to the wrong woman. I was about to be finished with him once and for all after our final performance, but there's another woman who actually felt a loss when Benny stopped seeing her. If you want to know who was angry enough to hit Benny from behind with his pitiful little acting award, you don't have to look any further than Amanda Lark. Do you even know who she is?"

I laughed with little conviction. "Oh, we know all about her. Funny, she told us that you were the one who probably killed Benny."

It was Sandra's turn to laugh. "What woman wouldn't try to transfer the blame to someone else in an effort to save face? Amanda was at the theater that night. Did you know that?"

"She told us that she was busy elsewhere," Moose said.

"And you believed her?" Sandra asked.

"Why should we believe you?" I asked her.

"Because I wasn't the only one who saw her here. Ask Garret if you don't believe me. She was so rowdy that he had to throw her out. The woman was drunk, plain and simple, and I'd be surprised if she even remembered killing Benny the next day when she came out of her stupor." She looked up, and my gaze followed hers. A man in a sleek warm-up suit approached us. "That's my boss. Now get out right now, before I sic Marcus on you both. He's very loyal to me, and he's not afraid to get his hands dirty."

"We're not afraid of him," Moose said.

"No? Maybe you should be."

"Come on," I said as I tugged at my grandfather's arm. "We're finished here, at least for now."

"I'd say for good," Sandra said.

"You might, but I wouldn't," I said as Moose and I left the gym.

"May I help you?" the manager asked as we approached him.

"We're still thinking about joining, but we're just not sure," I said. "My grandfather and I never make up our minds on the spur of the moment. Don't worry. We'll be back."

"I hope so," he said.

After we were in the parking lot heading for the truck, I said, "At least we have a personal invitation from the manager to come back now."

"Yes, but I don't think Sandra or Marcus will be too happy with us if we take him up on it, do you?"

"Maybe not, but that's going to be too bad. Do you believe her?"

"Are you referring to Sandra's attitude?"

"It's pretty bad, but that wasn't what I was talking about," I said. "I'm wondering if we should believe her claim that Amanda Lark was at the theater when Benny was murdered, despite what she told us about being busy somewhere else."

"There's only one way to find out," Moose said.

"Do you mean come right out and ask her?" I asked.

"I was thinking we should speak with Garret," my grandfather said. "I'd like a little proof before I tackle Amanda again."

"She doesn't intimidate you, does she?" I asked him with a grin.

"No, but I've never been all that fond of going after a bear with a BB gun. We need something bigger than

Sandra's word."

"You're right. It might be prudent to find out if it's true before we ask Amanda about it directly. Is there any chance that Garret will tell us the truth?"

"There's little doubt in my mind that he will," Moose said. "After all, what's he got to gain by lying to us? It's not like Amanda's one of his actors."

"You've got a point. He seems to treat them all like delicate flowers, doesn't he?"

"Too much so, for my taste," Moose said.

"To be fair, though, you were never a great fan of live theater."

"No, I'll leave that for you," he said. "Why don't we go pay a visit to Garret at his jewelry store? I doubt that he'll be willing to make a scene there, especially if there are any customers shopping on the scene."

"If there aren't, maybe I can drum one up to help us out," I said as I reached for my cell phone.

"Who are you going to call?" Moose asked.

"I thought I'd ask my favorite attorney if she'd like to do a little shopping on our behalf," I said as I called Rebecca Davis.

My best friend picked up on the second ring. "Hey, are you busy right now?"

"Victoria! I happen to have an hour free. Why, what did you have in mind?"

"How'd you like to go jewelry shopping?" I explained my idea to her, and she was delighted by it.

"It sounds wonderful. I've been meaning to pick up a new set of pearl earrings for ages, so this will be a perfect excuse."

"You don't really have to *buy* anything," I said. "You're mostly going to be there as window dressing."

"Nonsense. You know how much I hate window-shopping. If I go, I'm going to buy."

"That's fine. Just don't do it on my account, okay?"

She laughed, a sound I'd loved dearly since we'd both

been kids. "It won't be, you can bank on that. Shall we go together, or should I just meet you over there?"

"It will look better if it doesn't appear that we planned it," I said.

"Am I allowed to even speak to you, or is this deep cover?" Rebecca asked. I swear, I could hear her smile over the telephone.

"No, it's fine to say hello, but I'm hoping that if you're there, Garret will keep his temper in check. Maybe I can get him to answer a question or two without him dodging every time I ask him something."

"This sounds like fun. Thanks for thinking of me. I'll see you soon," she said.

"We're all set," I told Moose as I hung up. "Let's head over to the jewelry store."

"That's awfully nice of Rebecca to pretend to shop for you," Moose said as we headed across town.

"She made it perfectly clear that she's not doing it for me," I answered with a smile. "I honestly believe that she's going to enjoy it more than we are."

"It wouldn't surprise me in the least," Moose said.

Five minutes later, we pulled into the jewelry store's parking lot, and sure enough, Rebecca's car was already there.

It was time for us to question Garret about what Sandra had just told us, and to see if Amanda Lark had been elsewhere like she'd told us, or if she'd lied and had been at the theater when her recent ex-boyfriend had been murdered.

Rebecca winked at me as I walked through the door of the jewelry store. "Fancy seeing you here, Victoria," she said with a broad grin. In my opinion, it was way over the top, but then again, what could I expect from the rascal? She loved acting, and it was a wonder that she wasn't a member of the local troupe herself. "How are you?"

"I'm fine," I said as I smiled in Garret's direction, and then I returned my attention to Rebecca. "Have you found anything interesting yet?"

"Actually, there are *two* pairs of earrings I'm deciding between," she said. "Who knows? I might just get them both."

"Don't let me interrupt your shopping, then," I said. "Moose and I are here to speak with Garret."

"About jewelry?" she asked.

"No, I'm afraid not," I said. "I'll talk to you about it all later."

I turned to Moose and I said, "There he is. Let's go."

We approached Garret, who didn't look all that happy to see us. "I heard what you just told Rebecca, and I should warn you both right up front that if you're not here to shop, I'm not interested in talking to you. I've made up my mind, and it's final, so there's no use trying to change it."

"I understand," I said. I could see Moose's eyeballs nearly bulging as I said it, but he should have known me better than that. I wasn't about to give up that easily. "Moose, let's go get Rebecca and take her out to lunch. I'm sure if she really wants to buy something here, she can come back later if she has the time."

My grandfather nodded. "That's an excellent idea. The three of us could go to Union Square and eat at that Italian restaurant you're always talking about. I hear they have some pretty fine jewelry shops there as well." He turned to the jeweler and smiled at Garret. "It was nice seeing you again, Mr. Wilkes."

"Hang on. There's no reason to be hasty," Garret said. I knew that he loved every sale that he made, and the idea of Rebecca's money walking out the door without him snagging some of it was too much of a temptation for him. Knowing Rebecca, she might just buy both pairs of earrings anyway, but he didn't have to know that. "Now, what was it you wanted to know?"

"It's simple enough, really," I said. "We understand that you had an altercation with Amanda Lark at the theater the night Benny was murdered. Is that true?"

"I don't like to spread gossip or rumors," he said.

I doubted that was true at all. Maybe all he needed was a little push. "You wouldn't be. This won't go any further than between the three of us, unless we're forced to tell the sheriff about it. If that happens, you'd rather he hear from us than you, wouldn't you?"

Garret nodded, and it was clear that he'd had his share of Sheriff Croft already. It didn't really surprise me. I knew that the sheriff could be a doggedly determined man when he was on a case, and there was no doubt that he'd already been pressuring Garret, as well as his other suspects.

"I suppose so," Garret said, still hedging a little.

It was time to play my last card. "Unless you're the one who left that note at my house last night, I can probably keep the sheriff off your back, at least for now."

"What are you talking about?" he asked as he glanced over at Rebecca. She was showing no sign of impatience, and I wondered just how long she could pretend to be mesmerized by two pairs of earrings.

"Never mind. So, are you going to tell us about Amanda, or do we need to call Sheriff Croft and tell him that you're not cooperating?"

I fully realized that the sheriff would be baffled if I made that particular telephone call, but Garret didn't know that. "It's true. She was backstage where she didn't belong. She was drunk, so I ended up throwing her out. I couldn't afford to have my actors upset before a performance, you see."

"How did she take that?" Moose asked.

"About like you'd expect. She wasn't very happy with me, and I have a hunch that hasn't changed since Benny was murdered."

"Why didn't you tell us this the last time we spoke?" I asked the director/producer.

"I didn't want to be the one who dragged Amanda Lark into this," he said. "And I don't want her to know that I told you what happened, either. The woman can be all kinds of nasty when she puts her mind to it. I've been around some rough crowds in my life, but Amanda Lark chills me with her demeanor. I don't want to be looking over my shoulder for the next month waiting for her to retaliate, so I'd appreciate it if you'd keep my name out of it."

"We'll do what we can," I said. "Is there anything else that you've forgotten to tell us?" I asked. "Now would be a great time to come clean."

"No; that's it. I swear it. Now, if you'll excuse me, I've got a customer."

He started toward Rebecca, and I looked at her and nodded my head. I knew that we weren't likely to get much more out of Garret, and if my best friend wanted to exit now without buying anything, it was the perfect opportunity for her to do so.

She clearly had other plans, though. "Tell me, Mr. Wilkes, what kind of deal can you make me if I buy both pairs of earrings on the spot? Don't try to highball me, either. I may be an attorney, but I know the value of a dollar, so you'd better make your opening salvo count." Rebecca winked broadly at me as Garret started to stammer, and I knew that she was happy to be in her element. Rebecca would barter in businesses that others said couldn't be done, but I knew better after watching her over the years. Garret Wilkes had better count the change in his pocket and his fillings after my best friend left.

"Do we need to go back in and save her?" Moose asked me once we were outside again.

"If you ask me, Garret is the one who needs saving. There's no way that I'd ruin Rebecca's entertainment. She lives to haggle. No, we need to get over to the furniture outlet and see what Amanda Lark has to say for herself. I'm wondering if we should call the sheriff first, though. He has a right to know what we found out."

"Maybe after we speak with her ourselves first," Moose said. "After all, I hate generating a good lead and then just handing it over to him."

"I know exactly what you mean, but as soon as we talk to her, we have to call him. You agree with that, don't you?"

"I suppose," Moose said. "Do you think she killed him, especially after being caught at the theater like that?"

"What if she *already* killed him, and was just trying to get away?" I asked.

"Wouldn't she use the outside door, if that were the case?"

"Not if she panicked," I said.

"Funny, but Amanda Lark doesn't seem the sort to panic to me."

"You've got a point, but then again, we've never murdered anyone, so it's hard to say how we'd react, let alone try to predict her behavior. What it boils down to is that we need to talk to her directly and see how she reacts to our questions."

"She's not going to be happy; that's how she's going to react," Moose said with a crooked grin. "Next question."

"I don't know. She might surprise us both."

"She might, but I doubt it." We got into his truck, and Moose drove to the outskirts of town where the furniture outlet was located. I wasn't all that thrilled about going back inside. The place creeped me out.

But it turned out that I didn't have to go in after all.

Amanda Lark was out front smoking a cigarette and looking for all the world like she was ready to take on the world in a knife fight with her bare hands.

I hoped Moose parked the truck so that it was ready for a quick getaway, just in case we needed it.

"Hey, Amanda," I said as Moose and I approached. "Can we have a minute?"

She ground the cigarette on the pavement with the toe of her shoe. "If it's all the same to you, I'd really rather not," she said.

"It might be better if you talk to us out here rather than in there," Moose said, adding a nice ominous tone to his voice.

"Better for me, or for you?" she asked. There wasn't a hint of warmth in her voice, not that it surprised me any.

"For all of us," I said. "Why didn't you tell us that you were at the theater the night Benny was murdered? You said that you were busy elsewhere, but that wasn't true, was it?"

Amanda shook her head in disgust. "That lying little weasel. He promised to keep his mouth shut, but I can see what his word is worth."

"Who are you talking about?" I asked.

"Garret Wilkes, as if you didn't know," she said.

"Actually, someone else told us that you were there," Moose said. Technically it was true, but it nicely hid the fact that Garret had confirmed the information for us.

"They're all a bunch of blabbermouths," she said. "Sure, I was there. Big deal. I didn't see Benny; Garret saw to that. I tried his dressing room door, but it was locked. I knocked three or four times, but he never answered. I never had a chance to knock again. Garret threw me out, along with a few of his football-playing bodyguards. He'd better have them with him the next time I see him, or it's not going to turn out so well for that fancy-pants director, I'll tell you that."

"So, why did you lie to us?" Moose asked calmly.

"I knew you'd jump to the wrong conclusion if I told you the truth," she said harshly. "Besides, neither one of you is a cop. I was under no obligation to tell you the truth."

"Amanda, you just admitted that you lied to us when you told us that you weren't at the theater the night that Benny was murdered. Are there any more lies you'd like to clear up while we're here?" I asked her.

"I don't like your tone of voice, Victoria," Amanda said.

"Then, we're even, because we hate being lied to," Moose said.

"The way that you two nose around, I figured that you'd be used to it by now," Amanda said as she turned away from us. "The main thing I said still stands. I didn't kill Benny. It doesn't matter where I was or what I was doing as long as that's the truth, and it is, believe it or not."

"Help us believe you," I said.

"Sorry, but that's not my problem." The front door opened, and an older man leaned out. He didn't say a word, but he tapped his wrist twice, even though he wasn't wearing a watch.

"I've got to go," Amanda said. "I can't afford to lose this job."

Once she was inside, Moose asked, "Should we go in and keep grilling her? You never even had a chance to ask her if she wrote that note."

"I doubt it's her style. If my porch had been set on fire, Amanda would be my top candidate, but a note seems a little mild for her taste."

"Even if it were pinned to the door-jam with a bloody ice pick?" Moose asked.

"It was paint, not blood, remember?" I asked.

"From the pictures you showed me, it sure looked like blood. Where do we go now? We're burning through our suspects at a pretty fierce clip."

"I think we should go back to the diner for now," I said. "We need to let them all stew a little before we question them again."

"Aren't you afraid that things might escalate to something more than a warning if we don't wrap this up quickly?" my grandfather asked.

"I'm afraid that it's a risk we're going to have to take," I said. "There is something that we're missing; I just know it. I can't put my finger on it, though."

"Try not to think about it. That's the best chance you've got that it will come to you."

"I really don't have much choice, do I?" I asked. "What do you say? Should we go back to The Charming Moose?"

"Why not?" he asked. "I wouldn't mind grabbing a bite with my wife."

"Tell you what. You can have lunch with her, and then I get to eat with Greg. Is that a deal?"

"It is," Moose said, and then he put his arm around me before we got into his truck. "Keep the faith, Victoria. We'll figure this one out yet."

"We'd better," I said. I wasn't so sure, but having Moose's reassurance didn't hurt matters.

Chapter 11

"We didn't expect to see you back so soon," Martha said happily as we walked back into The Charming Moose. "Have you both already worn your welcomes out all over town?"

"Just about," Moose said as he wrapped his wife up into his arms. "Did you miss us when we were gone?"

"Well, half of you, anyway," she said with a smile.

"I'm not even going to ask which half you missed," Moose said as he kissed her soundly.

"Good. I'm not sure that your ego could take it. I assume the investigation isn't going all that well. Am I correct?"

"You are. How did you know?" I asked her.

"You're back, aren't you? Don't worry. You'll figure this out."

"I just wish I had your faith in us," I said. The pep talks were fine, but what we really needed was to solve this murder.

"The Charming Moose," I said as I answered the phone by the cash register an hour later. We'd had a steady supply of customers, but we weren't setting any sales records. Still, it wasn't the end of the world. I knew that we'd somehow manage to make enough to stay afloat for another month. At least we had so far.

"This is Amanda Lark," she said on the other end of the line, and all thoughts of profits and losses leapt from my mind.

"Hello, Amanda. What can I do for you?"

"First off, I want to apologize."

I nearly dropped the telephone as she said it. "I'm sorry.

What was that?"

"I'm sorry. I've been on edge since Benny was murdered, but I had no right to take it out on you, okay. Don't ask me to say it again, because twice is about all that I can take."

"It's completely understandable," I said to her. Maybe Amanda had some civility in her after all.

"There's one other thing. I've been thinking about our conversation, and it's weighing on my mind. I wasn't entirely forthcoming with you and your grandfather earlier."

"How so?" I asked.

"Before you jump to any conclusions, I didn't lie to you. But there's something you probably should know."

It was fairly clear by her hesitation that she didn't want to share this information with me, but if that was the case, why had she called me in the first place? I decided that I could wait her out if I had to, so I stayed on the line, though I didn't add anything to the conversation.

"Victoria, are you still there?" she asked.

"I'm just waiting to hear what you've got to say," I said. "That will be seven dollars and thirty-four cents," I added to Kimberly Weems when she presented her check.

"What? Why should I pay you to hear something that I've got to say?"

"Sorry. I was talking to a customer," I explained.

"If you're busy, we can always talk later," Amanda said.

"No. Hold on. I'll get someone else to take over here so we can talk." I waved to Ellen, our morning and early-afternoon server, and then I pointed to the phone.

She came over quickly and reached for the receiver. "Who is it?"

"Sorry, I didn't make myself very clear," I said as I put the phone on my shoulder. "Could you watch the register for a minute? I won't be long."

Ellen looked disappointed, but she nodded her agreement. "Take your time."

"Thanks. You're a lifesaver," I said as I stepped away.

I'd been meaning to replace the old phone with one without the cord, but so far, I kept forgetting to do it.

"Amanda, are you still there?" I asked.

"Yes, but I don't have long. My boss is going to kill me if he finds out that I'm using the business phone for a personal call."

"Go on. You have my full attention."

"The other night when Benny was killed, I saw something at the theater that I didn't tell you about earlier. I'm still not sure that I know what it means, but I thought I'd better tell you, just in case the information is useful."

"What did you see?" I asked her.

"I'm not sure if anyone told you, and it's not like I'm not proud of it myself, but I'd had too much to drink that night, and after Garret threw me out of the theater, I didn't go straight home. As a matter of fact, I doubt that I could have, even if I'd wanted to. The liquor must have caught up to me as I was rounding the corner of the building, and I thought I was going to lose my supper right then and there. I leaned against the building in the shadows for I don't know how long, and after a while, things started to get better. I was about to make my way home when a movement caught my eye, so I stayed in the shadows to see if I could tell who it was. I was in no mood to talk to anyone, or let someone else see me the way I was feeling at the time. As I watched, someone popped his head around from the back. It was just for a moment, but I saw him, and it won't do him any good for him to try to deny it."

"Who was it exactly that you saw?" I asked.

"Fred Hitchings," she said quickly. "He was up to something; there's no doubt in my mind. I started to creep down the alley to see exactly what he was doing, but when I turned the corner, he was gone, vanished into thin air."

"Amanda, Fred had several bit parts in the play before anything ever happened to Benny. It's perfectly natural that he'd be at the theater during the opening night of the production."

"Sure, that explains what he'd be doing inside, but what was he doing *outside*? And where did he go? I went back the next day, and there are only four doors he could have ducked into, and one of them was Benny's dressing room."

"What about the other three doors?" I asked.

"I checked with Harvey Springs, the janitor there, and he told me that two of the doors were to dressing rooms, though one was never used, one was to the main corridor in back, and the fourth was to a storage area where they keep their props and supplies."

"So, he could have gone through any of them, and you wouldn't have known which one he chose," I said.

"That's true, but if he killed Benny, he'd know that door was unlocked. Don't you see?"

"It's a possibility," I said.

"Victoria, what if Benny was still alive at that point? Fred could have gone inside to kill him, and I didn't do a thing about it. In a way, that makes it my fault as much as it is Fred's."

"You can't blame yourself for that," I said. "Amanda, you didn't swing that trophy at Benny's head, did you?"

"No, of course not," she said quickly.

"Then you didn't have anything to do with it," I said firmly.

"I wish I felt that way," she said, "but I can't let myself off the hook so easily."

"There are too many ifs right now to say with any certainty who killed Benny," I said. "Don't jump to any conclusions until we find out exactly what happened."

"How do I do that? Anyway, I thought it was only fair that you knew what I saw. If I were you, I'd have another chat with Fred Hitchings."

"We plan to," I said. "Is there anything else that might help us?"

"No, I swear it. That's all I know."

"Thanks for calling," I said as I started to hang up.

"Find whoever killed him, would you?"

"We're doing our best," I said.

After I hung up the phone, Ellen said, "Can you take over now?"

"Sorry about that," I said. "I didn't mean to be so long."

"That's okay. I just hate to keep folks waiting for their food," Ellen replied.

"They shouldn't have to," I said. "I'll help you deliver the orders. After all, it was my fault you couldn't do it in the first place."

"That would be great," she said. "Just leave Fourteen for me, okay?"

I glanced over and saw Wayne Vincent sitting there. He and Ellen had been playing cat and mouse when it came to their mutual crushes, and I wondered if either one of them would ever do anything about it. "Are you sure? I don't mind serving Wayne myself," I said, trying to hide my smile.

"I'm positive," she said.

"Okay, suit yourself." As I walked by his seat, I smiled brightly and said, "Ellen will be right with you."

"Don't worry about me. I've got all the time in the world," he said with a grin.

"You might think so, but I wouldn't take *too* long, if I were you," I said.

Wayne looked at me oddly, and then Ellen brushed me away with her apron. "There are folks stacking up at the register, Victoria," she said.

I looked over to see old Mrs. Clarenton teetering toward the register, and judging by her pace, she might get there by closing tonight, or she might not. "I'll take care of it," I said with a smile as I walked back to my usual position by the register.

"How was everything today, Mrs. Clarenton?" I asked as I rang up her bill.

"Wonderful, as always. That husband of yours sure knows how to cook."

"I'll tell him that you enjoyed your meal," I said as I handed her back her change.

"You be sure to," she said, and then she started her trek back to her car. I held the door open for her, and as I watched her make her way to her car, I couldn't believe who I saw heading straight for the front door of the diner.

It appeared that Fred Hitchings was going to save me the trouble of tracking him down.

Grabbing my cell phone, I held my breath waiting for Moose to answer, but it ended up going to voicemail. At the sound of the beep, I said hurriedly, "Moose, this is Victoria. I don't know where you are or what you're doing, but you need to get over here. I've got a couple of new developments that you need to know about."

"I don't care who you're talking to," Fred said as he entered through the front door. "This is important. We need to talk."

"I don't doubt that we do," I said. "Come on inside."

Fred just shook his head as he stood there blocking the exit. "If you don't mind, this needs to be in neutral territory."

I pointed to a nearby bench that some folks liked to use to picnic in nice weather. "How about over there? I should warn you, though; I can't wander off too far. I'm needed inside."

"That's fine," he said, and we made our way to the bench. It was still close enough to the diner for me to retreat if I needed to, but I was pretty certain that I could handle Fred.

Then again, maybe Benny had felt the same way, to his eternal regret. I vowed to keep my eyes open, and at the first sign of trouble, I was going to race into the diner. I didn't care how it looked, either. Being safe was what mattered now.

"What can I do for you, Fred? Did you come by to confess?" It was a bold move, and one that I hoped I didn't regret later, but it was worth a shot.

"What are you talking about, Victoria? Confess to what?"

"Killing Benny, of course. I've got an eyewitness who

placed you at the back of the theater around the time that
Benny Booth was murdered."

"Of course I was there," he said with obvious disgust. "I
may have been his understudy, but I was in the play in my
own right myself. I had every reason to be there."

"Inside the theater, yes, but I've recently spoken to
someone who saw you outside near Benny's dressing room
door."

Fred shook his head. "Who is this supposed
eyewitness?"

· "I'd rather not say until I need to reveal their identity," I
said, being careful to keep Amanda's gender out of it. "Do
you care to comment?"

Fred smiled softly. "It was all one big mix-up. I was in
the prop room looking for a briefcase I could use in my first
scene. Someone grabbed mine, and I needed it for the play.
While I was in the prop room, some idiot closed the door,
and the light bulb in there has been burned out for months. I
couldn't see my way around, and when I found the back
door, I opened it for some light. It didn't do much good,
though, so I stepped outside to look at the briefcase I'd
found, and I was out there just long enough for it to close on
me. Before I knew what was happening, I was locked out of
the theater."

"Is that when you decided to use Benny's dressing room
door to get back in?" I asked.

"That's the thing. I didn't," he explained. "As a matter
of fact, I never even *tried* his door, so I couldn't even say if it
was locked or not just then."

"How did you get back inside in time for the play, then?"
I asked.

"I used the other dressing room door. It was open a bit,
so I slipped inside, and no one was the wiser. At least that's
what I thought at the time. Apparently someone saw me, but
I can't imagine who it might have been. The killer, maybe?"

That was an intriguing thought, one I hadn't even
considered given the nature of the admission. "Fred, whose

door did you go through?"

"That's why I'm here. I know I should have told you before, but I didn't want to point fingers at anyone. I need to tell somebody, though. I walked into Sandra Hall's dressing room, and then I made my way out into the hallway and got ready for my first scene."

"Didn't anyone say something to you when you barged in there?" This was the perfect opportunity to find out if what Sandra and Marcus had told me was true.

"No, I was ready to apologize, but I didn't have to. The room was empty."

"*No one* was there?" I asked. "Are you certain?"

"Positive," he said. "I thought it odd at the time that Sandra was gone, but I didn't really give it much thought. The more I thought about it, though, the more I realized that she could have gone next door through the back way, killed Benny, and then made it back to her dressing room without anyone knowing what she'd done."

"It sounds as though it's a possibility," I said. "Have you told the sheriff this?"

"No, I'm on my way there now. I just thought that you should know."

"Thanks, I appreciate that," I said as Ellen came outside.

"Victoria, is everything all right?"

"It's fine," I said.

"Greg was just wondering where you'd gotten off to, and I didn't see you leave," she said.

"I'll be inside in a minute," I said.

"Okay," she replied, but she didn't look all that sure about it.

"You might as well go on in," Fred said. "That's all I had to tell you. Watch your back around that woman, Victoria. Sandra might look pretty and harmless, but that woman's got a mean streak as wide as a river."

"I'll do that," I said. "Thanks for coming by."

After Fred Hitchings left, I had to wonder about my list of suspects. It seemed that nearly all of them had cast pointing fingers in other directions, and the case was muddled more now than it had been from the beginning. It was almost as though it was a concerted effort on all of them to stymie our investigation.

Well, it wasn't going to work. Moose and I would press on until the killer was found.

I just didn't have a clue as to what we should do next. Maybe Moose would.

At least that was my only hope at the moment.

"Can you watch the register again?" I asked Ellen. "It won't take a minute. I promise."

"Go on, take your time," she said. I looked over and saw that Wayne was gone, though I didn't know if that had anything to do with her willingness to watch the register for me or not.

I grabbed my cell phone and found an empty booth away from our customers. I still had the gym's number in memory, and as I dialed it, I found myself hoping that Sandra didn't answer it.

I was in luck. It was Marcus.

After I identified myself, I said, "Marcus, I have one more question for you, and then I'll leave you alone."

"For good?" he asked. Evidently I hadn't made too good an impression on the man, if he was that eager to get rid of me.

"How about for now? Is that good enough?" I asked.

"What is it?" he asked grumpily. "I may or may not answer it after I hear it."

"You told me earlier that you were in Sandra's dressing room the entire time everyone was backstage, and just before she went onstage."

"Yes, it's true. I was there."

"Are you sure you didn't step out for ten seconds? Maybe to use the restroom, or something else you might have forgotten about since?"

"I was there the entire time," he said emphatically. "You can bet on it."

"Did you see anyone try to come in or out while you were there, from either door?"

"The *only* person I saw was that fool telling me that Sandra was due on the stage in five minutes. I muttered that she wasn't there, but I don't think the man heard me. Why do you want to know?"

"I have my reasons," I said. "Thanks."

"Aren't you going to tell me anything?" he asked.

I chose to ignore the question and hung up. With any luck, he wouldn't even realize that I'd heard his question.

"I've got it now. Thanks," I told Ellen as I looked at the clock. "You've got twenty minutes left on your shift, but I worked you extra hard today. Why don't you go ahead home, and I won't punch you out until two. How does that sound?"

"Are you sure?" Ellen asked. "It would be perfect. I could stop off at the store and pick up a box cake mix and a dozen eggs without dragging the kids to the store with me."

"Making a cake, are you?" I asked with a smile.

"Actually, it's a dozen cupcakes for the bake sale tomorrow," she said. "Your husband has been kind enough to donate two of his pies to the cause, and he's even offered to deliver them himself. He's a good man."

"Thanks. I think so. Off you go now, before something comes up here."

"It's warm enough out. I won't even go in back for my coat." She was gone before I could stop her, not that I blamed her one bit. Time off was rare enough, and I knew that she would make good use of it.

I didn't mind. Jenny wasn't due in until four, but I could manage well enough by myself until then. If not, I could always call Martha back.

In the meantime, I'd wait on my customers, check them out at the register, and in my downtime, I'd try to figure out which man had lied to me this afternoon, Marcus Jackson or Fred Hitchings. One of them hadn't told me the truth, since they *both* couldn't have been in Sandra's dressing room without one of them seeing the other. It was real progress, even though I didn't know which one was lying, and which one wasn't. All I had to do was to prove the liar, and then carry on the investigation from there. It didn't necessarily make the liar the killer, but it wouldn't hurt my investigation with Moose to discover which one of them had something to hide.

Chapter 12

I thought about calling my grandfather, but before I could dial the number, the man himself walked in, with Martha in tow.

"Victoria, we need to talk," he said. "I've been thinking about our list, and I'd like to run some ideas past you."

"I need to talk to you, too. Why don't you let me go first?" I asked after I kissed my grandmother. "We won't be long. I promise."

"Oh, I'll be fine until you are," she said. "Where do we stand?"

I brought her up to date on our customers and their current status, and then Moose and I went back to the same booth where I'd been sitting earlier.

"What's up?" Moose asked.

I quickly told him everything I'd uncovered since I'd seen him last. He whistled softly under his breath, and then he said, "You've been busy, haven't you?"

"They all came to me," I said. "I swear I didn't go looking for any of them."

"Easy, Victoria. I approve. I've been beating my head against the wall driving around town trying to figure this out, but I haven't made a bit of progress. This is good news."

"Only if we can figure out who's lying to us, *and* if the same person is the killer," I said. "Those are two mighty big ifs."

"Maybe so, but at least it's something. Do you think one of them left that note on your door, or are we dealing with someone else entirely?"

"I believe the murderer is the same person who left the note, but I don't have any proof to back it up," I said.

"Don't worry about that. We'll find the proof after we

figure out who killed Benny," Moose said.

"I'm not sure that the police would approve of our investigation methods," I replied.

"They have their rules, and we have ours. Just how are we going to manage figuring out who's lying to us?"

"I confess, I don't have a clue. There are still way too many variables in this case, and we still have too many suspects. We have to remember that there's a good chance that Marcus and Fred's conflicting alibis could easily *both* turn out to be red herrings. As for Amanda, she's been a little *too* cooperative lately, and I just don't trust Garret. None of these issues necessarily point to the killer, but I surely seem to have a lot of theories dancing around in my mind. Right now, as far as I'm concerned, any of them could have done it."

"If you have any ideas about how we might go about eliminating a few of our suspects, I'd love to hear what you have to say," Moose said.

"Sorry. I haven't had any more luck than you have in that department. At this point, I honestly don't know what we're going to do."

"Are they putting on the play again tonight?" Moose asked.

"No, the theater was already booked for a magic act, so they've just got tomorrow night's performance before they close," I said.

"It's not a very long run, is it?"

"Given that the cast is full of amateurs, I have a feeling that it's long enough. Why do you ask? Do you have something in mind?"

"A little pot stirring might be in order," Moose said.

"I recognize that twinkle in your eye. You're up to no good, aren't you?"

"And if I am?" he asked.

"Then, I want in on it," I said firmly.

"That's my girl. Why don't we leave the diner in the capable hands of your husband and my wife, and we'll try to figure out the most effective way to rile folks up around here."

"That sounds like the best plan we could have, given how stymied we are at the moment with actually detecting anything."

Moose grinned and touched the tip of my nose with his forefinger, just as he'd done when I'd been a young child. "You know that, and I know it as well, but the killer has no idea that we're stumbling around in the dark, the same as the police department seems to be doing."

"We suspect that, but we don't know it," I said. "To be honest, I wouldn't mind if Sheriff Croft solved this one himself. As far as I'm concerned, the sooner we can get this cloud away from our family's good name, the better."

"Agreed. Let's take a drive and brainstorm, shall we?"

"I'm game if you are," I said.

As we drove around town, Moose and I must have thrown out a dozen ideas apiece on how to catch this killer given what we knew at the moment, but we weren't able to come up with anything that we both thought might work.

"We should just be done with it and leave each one of them a note with my answer," I said, half in jest. "If anyone challenges me directly about it, we'll know who did it."

"I thought about that, too, but it probably won't work. Everyone is too closely tied together in this blasted case. I'm afraid that they'll all compare notes, and then we're sunk. The killer will know that we're just taking a stab in the dark."

"Hang on a second," I said. "Let's not dismiss it that quickly. When you think about it, only Marcus and Sandra are likely to talk to each other, and we can tailor whatever we say in their notes so if they do compare, it won't give us away."

"I don't know," Moose said. "It's kind of risky, isn't it?"

"You were the one who said we needed to stir the pot," I reminded him. This should certainly accomplish that."

"You're right. Let's go back to the diner and brainstorm about what the note should say," my grandfather said as he turned the truck around and headed back to The Charming Moose.

"Martha, would you mind running the register a little longer?" I asked as we walked into the diner. It was a slow day, something I was thankful for, and Jenny had just come on duty. "I'm sure that the worst of the rush is over for now."

"Do whatever you need to do," Martha said.

"Thanks," I answered, as Moose offered thanks of his own with a quick kiss.

"We'll be over there if you need us," he said, pointing to an empty booth away from the diners.

"I'm sure I'll be fine," she said.

I reached down and pulled out a notebook I kept under the register. A pen was clipped to it, and after getting tea for me and coffee for Moose, we started thinking about what we should say.

After an hour, we had a note that worked pretty well. The message read, printed in block letters, I WON'T BACK OFF. CONFESS!

"It's kind of aggressive, isn't it?" Moose asked. "Do you think it's too much? We don't want the killer coming after you."

"I don't think we have any choice at this point. I've been thinking about it, and I think we need to pick either Sandra or Marcus to get one of our notes, but not both of them. Otherwise, they'll compare them, and then they'll *know* that we're bluffing."

"I see your point, but which one gets the note?"

"It has to be Marcus, don't you think?" I asked.

"Why? It sounds as though Sandra had as much reason to want Benny dead as her boyfriend did."

"I know, but chances are good that either Marcus or Fred lied to us about where they were when Benny was murdered, if we are to believe Amanda's story. Actually, it occurs to me that we should believe her, anyway. Fred confirmed that he went into the theater through Sandra's dressing room, so from Amanda's point of view, what she saw was true. I know that Sandra *could* have killed Benny, but I doubt that it will help us to single her out at this point, since as far as we know, *she* never lied to us. Let's go with Marcus and see where that leads us."

"Agreed," Moose said. "Would you like to print out the individual notes, or should I do it myself? I'm fairly decent at writing in block letters."

"Then, by all means, you do it," I said. The diner was starting to get busy, and Martha looked a little overwhelmed by it all, despite Jenny doing the majority of the work. "If you don't mind, I'm going to lend your wife a hand."

"I'm sure that she would appreciate it. Don't worry about me. I've got this covered."

I left him carefully printing out the first note, and I glanced at him from time to time as I walked past either taking orders, delivering food, or working the cash register.

When I walked past him later, there was a growing stack of notes in front of Moose, and as he closed the notebook, I asked, "Are you all finished?"

My grandfather gathered the loose notes up and smiled. "They're all taken care of. How should we deliver them? I don't think we should use an ice pick for each one."

"That might be a little *too* aggressive. I've got some generic envelopes in the office in back. I'll grab a handful, and you can address them to our suspects."

"We don't have time to mail them, Victoria," Moose said.

"I know that, but I don't want to leave the notes out somewhere so that *anyone* could read them. Once it gets dark, we need to make a little special mail run and hand-deliver them."

"It's going to have to do more than get dark," Moose said. "I think we should wait until midnight to hand these out. Otherwise, there's a risk that someone will see us doing it."

I thought briefly about how early I was going to have to get up the next morning, but this was more important than losing a little sleep. "Midnight it is," I agreed.

As I went into the kitchen to grab the spare envelopes from the office, Greg asked, "What's going on in the crime-solving business?"

"Well, we've got an idea, but I'm not sure how well it's going to work out," I admitted.

"I'm sure it will be great," Greg said.

"I wish I had your confidence in our abilities, but truth be told, Moose and I are struggling at the moment."

"Victoria, you worry too much. You'll figure it out," Greg said.

"Thanks," I answered. "By the way, Moose and I have a few errands to run."

"Go on. I'm sure that Martha and Jenny can handle things here on this end."

"The problem is that we can't start until midnight," I said.

"Good luck with that," Greg said with the hint of a laugh. "Just try not to wake me up as you leave or when you come back. I need my beauty sleep, you know."

"Not more than I do," I said.

My husband stepped away from the grill for a second and hugged me. It felt good being in his arms, if only for a few seconds, and the scents of burgers and fries that filled the air wrapped me in their warmth. I'd associate those smells with my husband's embrace long after he passed his spatula over to the next grill-master.

"Would it help any if I told you that you were more beautiful right now than the day I married you?" he asked softly.

"I'd know that you were lying, but yeah, it would help a lot."

Greg laughed as he pulled away and smiled at me. "You are one of a kind, Victoria."

"I surely hope so," I said. That hug did wonders for me. It was better than three glasses of tea and a hot shower, and I had a spring to my step as I walked back out into the dining room.

Moose smiled broadly at me. "Whatever you just got, I want some for myself."

"Greg just hugged me," I said. "I'm sure he'd be happy to oblige you, if you asked him nicely."

"I think I'll pass," Moose said, "as tempting as that sounds." He took the envelopes from me, and said, "Perfect. Now, should we do full names, or first names only?"

"Let's keep them casual and stick with first names," I said.

"Done and done," Moose said as he started on the first one.

I rang up a few bills and delivered some meatloaf to a customer, and when I got back to Moose, he'd finished his task and stuffed every envelope.

"Would you like me to hold onto those?" I asked.

"Thanks, but I figure if I take them home with me, you won't be tempted to deliver them early. I know how much you like your sleep."

"I'd never do that without you," I said.

"Well, just in case, let's keep temptation at arm's length, shall we?" He stood as his wife came over to join us. "Martha, are you ready to go home? I'm sure we can coax Greg into whipping something special up for us from the kitchen before we go."

"I'm certain of it, but I have a pot roast in the slow cooker that's due to come out in twenty minutes."

"Did you put extra carrots in like I enjoy?"

"Two bags worth," she said. "I'd never forget something like that."

Moose grinned. "I knew there was a solid reason I fell in love with you."

"I've got a hunch it was for more than my pot roast," Martha said with a laugh.

"Oh, so much more." As they started to walk out, Moose said, "I'll see you tonight, Victoria. Try to resist the temptation to go out sleuthing on your own in the meantime, okay?"

"I'll try," I answered.

"Where are you two going tonight?" Martha asked as they reached the door.

"I'll tell you later over carrots," he replied.

I hadn't even realized that Jenny had walked up beside me until she said, "I really want that some day."

"What's that?"

"What the two of them have," she said wistfully.

"There will be plenty of time for you to find it," I reassured her. "How are classes going this semester?"

"Not great, as a matter of fact. My favorite professor quit after one class, and my least favorite one took over for him. It's not going to be pretty, I'll tell you that."

"I'm sure you'll do fine. You always do."

With fingers crossed, Jenny said, "At least so far."

It was a relatively quiet evening, and when seven rolled around, I was ready to lock up for the night. After we let Jenny go, Greg and I closed the diner, going through a routine that we could both do in our sleep.

I stifled a yawn as I shoved the receipts and cash into the deposit envelope.

"Why am I so sleepy?" I asked Greg as he came out front.

"Probably because you've got a late-night errand to run tonight," my husband said with a grin. "Would you like to catch a quick nap before you go out with your grandfather?"

"No. As tempting as it sounds, I'd never get to sleep after we got back. I'll just have to tough it out."

"I made us meatloaf sandwiches," he said as he held up a bag. "I don't know about you, but I don't feel like cooking tonight."

"That sounds wonderful," I said.

After we got home, I set the table, and Greg and I dined on cold meatloaf sandwiches, chips, and milk. Some folks might have turned their noses up at such a dinner, but as far as I was concerned, it was a meal fit for royalty.

"Feel like a movie to pass the time until Moose comes by to pick you up?" Greg asked.

"That sounds great," I said, and we both settled in on the couch, me with my head tucked on Greg's shoulder.

We couldn't have been more than three minutes past the opening credits when I felt Greg shake my arm. "Hey, wake up, sleepyhead. Your grandfather just drove up."

I rubbed my eyes, and I then stared at the clock.

It was three minutes until midnight.

"How long was I asleep?" I asked him.

"It was a solid four hours, and from the sound of your snoring, I'd say that you must have really needed it."

"Why didn't you wake me up?" I asked as I stood and stretched.

He looked a little sheepish as he admitted, "Mainly because I fell asleep, too. I'm sorry you have to go out again tonight."

"Don't be," I said as I gave him a quick kiss, and then I headed for the door. "This needs to be done if we're going to make any progress in the case."

I watched as Moose mounted the steps, and then I pulled the front door open. "Are you ready to do a little mischief?" I asked him.

"I'm always ready for that," he said.

"Let me grab my jacket and we'll be off, then," I replied.

He looked at me carefully. "Victoria, did you take a nap?"

"Didn't you? It seemed to be a prudent thing to do."

Moose just laughed. "I can see how you might feel that way. Then again, I haven't worked the hours you do in donkey years."

"Do you have the envelopes with you?" I asked.

"They're in the truck," he said. "I don't suppose I could get a little coffee before we go, could I?"

Greg must have read his mind, because he came out of

the kitchen just as Moose finished making his request, and my husband had a pair of traveler's mugs with him, one in each hand. "I thought you both might need a little caffeine in your system to keep you going," he said.

"You are quickly becoming one of my favorite people in the world," Moose told Greg.

My husband smiled broadly. "If I'm on a list, that's the one I want to make. Safe hunting, and be careful tonight, both of you."

"This evening we're acting in stealth mode," my grandfather said. "If we do it right, no one will ever know that we were there."

"Then, by all means, do it right," Greg said.

"You don't have to wait up," I told my husband as we headed out the door.

"I know that I don't have to, but I will, nevertheless."

I gave him a quick kiss, and then I said, "See you soon."

"Be careful," he whispered in my ear. "I mean it."

"Always," I replied.

After we got into the truck and Moose started driving to our first drop-off, he took a long sip of coffee, and then he said, "I really like that fellow of yours."

"That's good. I'm rather fond of him myself," I said.

"It's awfully quiet out, isn't it?" Moose asked a few minutes later as we drove the nearly deserted streets of Jasper Fork. "I'm not used to seeing town at this time of night."

"Neither am I," Moose said. "I'm surprised there are as many folks out as we're seeing. Maybe we should wait a few more hours until we deliver our special mail."

"Moose, if I go back home, I'm going straight to bed, nap or no nap. I'm afraid that we're just going to have to take our chances."

"I know what you mean, and I agree with you. We just need to be extra careful."

"Agreed. So, who's first on our list? Did you get all of their addresses?"

"I did," he said proudly.

"That internet can be a pretty powerful tool, can't it?" I asked. Moose wasn't exactly a technophobe, but he hadn't fully embraced the information age yet, either.

"I'm sure that it is, but I used our phone book at home," he said. "It had all the information I needed, and I didn't have to reglove anything to find it."

"Reboot," I said, correcting him automatically. "As long as you got those addresses somewhere. Do you have a plan?"

"My dear old grandfather always taught me to go to the farthest place first and work my way back home, and I haven't found a reason to go against his advice yet."

I loved stories about my grandfather's grandfather, and I could never get enough of them. "He sounds as though he was a disciplined man."

"He was that, and as organized a fellow as I've ever met. Why, he had his socks arranged in his drawer by the year and month that he purchased them, and he always wore them in perfect rotation."

"Surely you're exaggerating," I said.

"I am not," Moose said. "He had my grandmother stitch little hash marks in the heel of each sock so he'd be able to tell them apart."

"How did she manage to put up with him for all those years?"

My grandfather laughed. "She loved him more than any woman ever loved a man, as far as I could tell, and I know from experience that allows you to let a great many things slide that would infuriate you otherwise."

"Are you saying that Martha has learned to put up with your idiosyncrasies over the years, and that she loves you in spite of them?"

"Perhaps even because of them," Moose said. "Enough of that, though. I've planned to visit our suspects in this order. Fred Hitchings is first, then it's Amanda Lark, Garret Wilkes, and finally Marcus Jackson. How does that sound to you?"

"Far be it for me to interfere with a man's well thought-out system," I said with a smile.

"Then that's what we'll do."

Chapter 13

"Moose, the light's still on," I said as we drove close to Fred Hitchings' house. "What should we do?"

"It's most likely just on a timer," my grandfather said as he pulled the truck to a stop a hundred feet after we passed Fred's house.

"Are you sure about this address?" I asked as I looked out the window.

"Positive," Moose said. "Why?"

"I expected more than this from a man who has so much money," I said. There wasn't exactly anything wrong with the house. I was sure that it would be fine for most folks, but it looked to be worth about the same as my place, and I ran a diner, not two car dealerships.

"What were you expecting, an estate?" Moose asked. "One way folks hold onto their money is not to spend it unnecessarily. If you ask me, I think more of Fred Hitchings after seeing his house than I ever did before. Do you have the notes?"

I held up the large folder as I nodded. "I do." I grabbed the roll of fresh gray duct tape. "Are you sure we shouldn't just tape these up with regular clear tape?"

"I've given it a lot of thought, and I believe the duct tape leaves more of a message," Moose said.

"Okay, I'll trust you on this one." I ripped off a piece neatly, and when Moose saw it, he shook his head.

"Let me have that," he said, and I handed the gray roll over.

Instead of trying to produce a neat edge, Moose intentionally tore a jagged piece, and then another, making my smooth edge vanish. "There, that's better. It looks a little crazier now, don't you think?"

"Sure, but is that the message we really want to send?"

"We're stirring the pot, Victoria. The crazier we can look, the better."

"Maybe we should redo the notes, too, then."

Moose studied his handiwork, and then he shook his head. "I kind of like what I've done. Besides, we can't overthink this. Do you want to put them up, or should I do it?"

"I will," I said. "I want you behind the wheel in case something goes wrong."

"What could possibly go wrong?" my grandfather asked with a smile.

"Let's not even think about that," I said.

"Are you ready?"

"As I'll ever be," I said as I started to get out of the truck. The cab light came on as the door opened.

"Sorry about that, Victoria," Moose said as he adjusted something on his dash. "That won't happen again."

"I hope not."

I looked back once I was near the front door, but I could barely make out the truck from there, let alone see that anybody was inside.

Taking a deep breath, I hurried the rest of the way to the front door.

The lights suddenly came on all around me, blinding me with their intensity. Was Fred on the other side of the door, watching me? No, the lights had to all be on motion sensors. Darting forward, I taped the note to the door, and then I turned and ran back to the truck as fast as I could. By the time I got to the truck, I was out of breath, but Moose had been watching me. The truck was already running, and he took off before my door was even closed all of the way.

"Do you think he saw me?" I asked between pants.

"I sincerely doubt it. If he had, I'm fairly sure he would have come racing out. Those outside lights had to be set with motion detectors. I didn't think about that as a possibility."

"I didn't either, and what's worse, my lights work the same way, so I should have at least considered the possibility that someone else had done it, too."

"How could we have avoided it?" Moose asked. "It's not as though Fred had security cameras set up on the porch. Or did he?"

"I didn't see anything, but then again, I was pretty focused on taping that note in place and getting out of there as fast as I could."

"We're probably safe, then," Moose said, but he didn't sound all that confident.

"I just hope we have more luck at the next house," I said.

"Does that mean that you're willing to keep doing this?" Moose asked, clearly surprised by my willingness.

"The theory's still sound," I said. "We need to see this through."

He patted my knee. "That's my girl. The rest shouldn't be that hard."

"Let's hope not."

By the time we finished delivering all of our notes, we had only one more close call. At Marcus Jackson's place, as I'd taped the note in place on his front door, what sounded like a pit bull started barking on the other side. If Marcus was home, it would get him there in no time. Once again, I raced for the truck, and Moose took off before a single light came on in the house.

"I'm glad that's over," I said as Moose drove me home. "I don't think I have the nerve to do that again."

"And now we wait," Moose said.

"I've been thinking about that," I said. "How are we going to know if we did any good at all with our little replies?"

"There are a couple of things we should keep a lookout for tomorrow," Moose replied. "I'd be interested to see if any of our suspects suddenly take off and leave town."

"Wouldn't doing that just make them look guilty?"

"Sure it would, but I'm counting on the fact that their self preservation instincts will be too strong to ignore."

"It would be great if whoever did it would just step up and confess," I said.

"There's another possibility that I'm beginning to worry about," Moose said. "The murderer might choose to fight back rather than leave town. You need to stay on your toes for the next few days."

"Surely the killer wouldn't be brazen enough to come after me."

"They threatened you, and you're returning the favor. It's a possibility that they might see that as an act of aggression."

"I didn't full consider that," I said.

"Maybe it would be better if you and Greg came over and stayed with Martha and me until this blows over."

"Thanks for the offer, but I'm not leaving my home. If I do that, then the killer will know that I'm running scared."

"If you don't, whoever killed Benny might do something more drastic than leave you a note next time," Moose said. "This could get dangerous really quickly."

"If someone comes after me, I'll be ready for them," I said, "but I'm not going to hide."

"Suit yourself," Moose said. "You're going to at least tell Greg about our talk, though, won't you?"

"The second I get home, I'll tell him everything," I said. "I'm not going to let anyone run me out of my own home, but there's no use being stupid about it, either. I'll be curious to see if any of our suspects come by the diner tomorrow."

Moose pointed to the clock. It read one forty-five, but until I saw it, I wasn't aware of just how late it really was. That must have been the adrenaline. "Today, you mean."

"It's going to be a brutal day, I can tell you that already."

"At least you're young," my grandfather said.

"Not as young as I used to be, but I'll manage."

We pulled up in front of the house, and I saw that, as promised, Greg was still up. At least he didn't have to go in until eleven. There might be time for him to catch up on most of the sleep he'd lost waiting up for me, but I was a lost cause. "I hope this works."

"What choice did we have?" Moose asked. "The pot has officially been stirred, wouldn't you say?"

"I would," I said as I leaned over and kissed his cheek. "Good night, Moose. Or good morning. Whatever fits."

"Sleep well, Victoria."

"Well, if not long," I said.

Greg opened the door, and I'd rarely been happier about having a home, and a husband who loved me. "How did it go?"

"As well as could be expected," I said. "We had a few close calls, but that just made things a little more interesting."

"Tell me all about it," he said. "I've got some of my special blend of hot cocoa waiting for you."

"That sounds great. I don't think I could swallow another sip of coffee or tea. Greg, Moose is worried about the killer coming here after me. He offered to put us up, but I turned him down. Is that all right with you?"

"That depends. What was your reason for saying no?"

"I won't have anyone running us out of our home, no matter what danger it might invite. Am I being foolish?"

"Victoria, you are a great many things, and most of them are good, but foolish is not a word I'd ever use to describe you. I'm with you."

"Are you sure? We could always go, if you'd rather," I said. I was beginning to wonder if I'd been right to rely so much on my pride. In the end when all was said and done, was staying put to make a point really worth risking our lives?

"Go if you feel like you have to, but I agree with what you said before. *I'm* not leaving."

I kissed him, and then I took a small sip of cocoa. "I'm not, either. Now, if you don't mind, I'm going to bed. I might not be able to get much sleep, but I'm going to at least try to get as much as I can manage."

"I'm right behind you," he said.

I'd worried a little about being able to fall asleep after all the excitement, but I dozed off before my head even hit the pillow. I was tempted to sleep in, but when the alarm clock rang the next morning, I felt nearly as good as if I'd had a full night's rest, instead of the abbreviated sleep I actually got.

It was a big day, and hopefully, Moose and I had lit a fire under the killer.

In their haste, maybe they'd make a mistake and reveal themselves.

If our plan worked as well as we hoped.

"Good morning, Sheriff," I said the next morning as Sheriff Croft came into the diner bright and early. I'd waved Ellen away so I could wait on him myself. If I got lucky, maybe he'd toss a crumb or two of information my way. "Can I get you something to eat?"

"That depends," he said as he walked to the counter, took a seat, pulled out the menu, and began to study it. His reading glasses kept slipping down his nose, and I wondered if they were new. After a moment, he closed the menu and asked, "Does your mother still make those cinnamon stick waffles she used to be famous for?"

"They're one of her specialties," I said.

"Good. I'll take an order of those, a side of crisp bacon, and some coffee."

"I'll get right on it," I said. "It's good to see you this morning."

"I was kind of hoping to get a second to chat with you," he said as he looked around. "But the place looks like it's pretty busy at the moment."

"Don't let them fool you. Most of our customers have already finished eating; they're just nursing their coffees until they have to go to work. I've got a little time to talk right after I place your order."

"That would be much appreciated," he said. Why was the man going out of his way to be pleasant and cordial with me? He wasn't necessarily rude most times, but he wasn't nearly as nice as he was being at the moment, either. Either he knew something, or he *wanted* to know something, and I knew better than to push him, either way.

"Order up," I told Mom as I slid it across the pass-through to her. "It's for the sheriff, so take your time."

"I can't promise anything," she said with a smile. "You know me. I pride myself on being lightning quick."

"I know, I know," I answered. "Just do what you can," I said as I added a wink.

I poured some coffee for the sheriff, and then I poured a little for myself, too. "Now, what would you like to talk about?"

He reached into his pocket, pulled out a sealed plastic evidence bag, and then he shoved it toward me. I knew the words printed there by heart, since I'd delivered that note, as well as three others just like it, the night before.

I pushed it back to him. "Where did you get that?"

"How many did you and Moose put out, Victoria?" he asked, his glance never straying in my direction.

"What are you talking about?"

"Is that how we're playing things now? Funny. I thought you prided yourself on cooperating with my investigations. Has something changed that I don't know about?"

He was right. This wasn't the time to be cute. I had given my word long ago that I wouldn't knowingly go against him in any of his investigations, and in return, he'd promised to look the other way sometimes when Moose and I pushed the boundaries a little too far. "Sorry; you're right. That was out of line. Last night a little after midnight, Moose and I taped one of those notes to the doors of each of our suspects, except one. Who got that one, and how did it end up in your hands so fast?"

"Why don't you let me ask all of my questions first, and if there's time, we'll get around to yours." It was clear that he was still not happy about my attempt to hold out on him.

"That's fine," I said. "What do you want to know?"

"Who got copies of this note?"

"Fred Hitchings, Marcus Jackson, Garret Wilkes, and Amanda Lark."

"Not Sandra Hall?" he asked.

"Why, should we have included her on our list?" I knew that it was a direct question, but I couldn't help myself.

"You're talking and I'm listening, remember?"

"Got it. We thought Marcus was a more likely suspect, given what we found out about him earlier, and we couldn't very well leave them both notes. They would have compared them straight away, wouldn't they?"

"Most likely. What did you uncover about Marcus?"

"He claimed that he was in Sandra's dressing room when Benny was murdered, but Fred Hitchings said he was there at the exact same time, and neither one of them saw the other. That means that one of them *has* to be lying."

"Are you telling me that they *both* came forward and shared their alibis with you and Moose? I find that hard to believe."

"I'm telling you the truth," I said, raising my voice a little more than I meant to. A few folks looked over in our direction, but they quickly feigned disinterest when I made eye contact with each and every one of them.

"Take it easy," Sheriff Croft said. "I'm not accusing you of anything. As it turns out, they told me the same thing. Do you have a feeling about which one of them might have been lying to you?"

"I keep going back and forth," I said. "It's tough proving where you weren't, isn't it?"

"That's why I make the big bucks," he said with the hint of a grin. Evidently he'd decided to forgive me and let me off the hook, which was a very good thing. I knew that Moose and I operated on the fringe without any authority to do so, and the sheriff could shut us down any time that he pleased. "What else do you know?"

"That it's a boat full of rats on a sinking ship," I said. "There's not a soul on our list who didn't try to throw another one under the bus at the earliest opportunity. We've been spinning our wheels, so Moose and I decided that what this case needed was a little pot stirring."

"Thus the notes," the sheriff said as he nodded. "This is a dangerous game you're playing with your life, here."

"Sheriff, I'm well aware that it's no game. We still have five suspects on our list, and not much to help us go on from here. Now, I've been as cooperative as I could be. Would you mind telling me if we're off-base at all with our list of suspects?"

"You've got the majority of them there. That's good work, Victoria. Both you and Moose should be proud of yourselves."

"Thanks. Are we leaving someone out, or do we have too many names on our list? You'd be doing us a huge favor if you'd share with us just a little."

He looked as though he were about to talk, and then the sheriff suddenly pointed to the pass-through window. "Is that my breakfast?"

"I'll check," I said. Sure enough, Mom had finished his meal in record time. I grabbed the plate, then the coffee pot, and I slid the food in front of him. As soon as I did that, I topped off his coffee, but I left my alone. "There you go," I said. "Enjoy."

"Thank you," he said, and then the sheriff lost himself in my mother's breakfast offering. I knew that a great many breakfast chains and frozen food manufacturers struggled to find the perfect recipe for their cinnamon waffle sticks, but they were never as good as my mother's were. The sheriff poured a little maple syrup on his plate, added a touch of brown sugar, and then he dragged the first stick through the mixture. I wished that Mom could see the smile on his face when he took that first bite. A smile exploded as he chewed, and I decided to respect the food and leave him alone, at least while he was eating.

I topped his coffee off once more, but for the most part, I left the man alone in peace to eat his breakfast. I doubted that he had a great deal of time to himself most parts of the day, and I just couldn't bring myself to push him for more information while he was eating.

The sheriff took a ten dollar bill out of his pocket and slid it under his plate as he stood. "Tell your mother that she hasn't lost her touch."

"I will, but she already knows that," I said with a grin. "Hang on. I'll get your change."

"The rest is for you," he said with a smile.

"For the service, or for leaving you alone?" I asked.

"Let's just say both reasons are equally valid," he said with a grin.

"Thanks, but as much as I appreciate the thought, I don't take tips here, since I run the place. Let me get you your change."

"Any chance that I could get a coffee to go while you're at it?" he asked.

"You bet," I said. I rang up his bill, and then grabbed a lidded cup and filled it up with fresh coffee. "There you go."

As he took his change and the coffee, I said, "I'm really sorry about holding out on you before. That was over the line."

"I'm not blaming you a bit, though I never would have approved of you doing it if you'd asked me about it first," he said. "For what it's worth, it wasn't a bad idea."

"Do you think it's going to work?"

"Well, nobody's taken off yet. I can't afford the manpower to watch all of my suspects around the clock, but I'll be curious to see how they act today. I'll try to keep an eye on you, but I can't make any promises about that, either."

The sheriff was almost out the door when he paused and looked back at me. In a soft voice, he said, "I got the note from Garret Wilkes. He told me to find out who did this, and when I did, to drive a stake through their hearts. He doesn't scare easy, that one."

"Do you think that makes him innocent?" I asked.

"I don't know that anyone could ever call him that, but no, I don't think he murdered Benny."

That was certainly news. "Why not?"

"He was being shadowed all night when the murder took place by a girl from the high school newspaper. She was doing a feature on him about what it was like to direct a play, and she never left his side."

Why hadn't Moose and I heard about this? I couldn't possibly think of a reason that Garret would want to hide it from us. Why hadn't he told us? "Are you sure about that? Every second is hard to account for," I said.

"She can do it. The girl not only took meticulous notes, but she recorded the entire time she was shadowing him. It makes for some fascinating viewing, especially when Garret threw Amanda Lark out of the theater."

"Is she still on your list as well?" I asked. I still felt the sting from missing such an important alibi from one of our main suspects, but then again, my grandfather and I didn't have the authority to *make* anyone talk to us. It was a wonder we got anything out of anybody at all.

"I really can't say," the sheriff said.

"Does that mean that you don't know?" I asked.

He grinned. "No, it just means that I can't say. Thanks again for breakfast."

"You're welcome. Thank you for the information."

"Isn't cooperation a grand thing?" he asked with a smile. "Keep me posted, Victoria."

"I'd ask you to do the same, but I don't have much hope in that happening," I said.

"Whoever said that you wouldn't have made a good detective?"

My, but he was in a good mood. Perhaps he was closer to finding the killer than my grandfather and I were. It shouldn't surprise me. Sheriff Croft had a great many more resources than we had, and more training as well.

Still, I would love to be the one who finally cracked the murder case.

I was reaching for Helen Murphy's bill when I noticed

the sad expression on her face. "Is something wrong, Mrs. Murphy?"

"As a matter of fact, there is."

"Was your breakfast unsatisfactory?"

"No, of course not," she said. "Your mother's a fine cook, Victoria, and she always has been. The problem is I can't believe that my favorite actor is dead."

I hadn't watched television or read a newspaper lately, and I wondered who Hollywood had lost. "I'm sorry for your loss," I said.

"Mr. Booth was a real treasure," she said, and I realized that she'd been talking about Benny. I had a difficult time believing that he'd been anyone's favorite, but it just showed that you could never tell when it came to taste. "You wouldn't happen to want an extra pair of tickets, would you? I just can't bring myself to go to the theater tonight."

"I'd love them," I said. I'd been hoping to see the last performance, but I hadn't held out much hope in acquiring tickets. Since Benny's murder, tickets to the play's final show had become the scarcest thing around Jasper Fork in years.

I reached for my purse, tucked under the register. "How much do I owe you?"

"I couldn't take a penny for them," she said. "It wouldn't be right profiting off such a tragic event."

"Really, I couldn't take them for free," I said. "Tell you what. At least let me buy breakfast for you, even though I'm cheating you, and we both know it."

"That would be lovely," Mrs. Murphy said as she handed the tickets over. "It's good to know that they'll go to a good home. I hope you enjoy the show tonight, Victoria."

"I'm happy to get the opportunity," I said.

The opportunity to see two of my suspects in action again was priceless. I tucked the tickets into my purse, and then I focused on my other diners.

I had a long time to go before the show tonight, and hopefully, I'd have a little more luck in the meantime eliminating one or two of the suspects still on my list.

Chapter 14

"Hi, Amanda. Fancy seeing you here," I said as one of my remaining four suspects walked into The Charming Moose.

"I've been hearing a lot about the place, so I thought I'd see what all of the fuss was about."

"Well, sit wherever you'd like," I said. "I'll be right with you."

I put on my best smile, and it clearly puzzled her a little.

She ordered black coffee and dry toast, and I felt guilty about charging her for such meager fare.

As I presented the bill a few minutes later, I asked, "Are you sure that I can't get you anything a little more substantial?"

"No, this is all I need," she said as she fumbled in her purse for money. Her handbag fell to the floor, and it just about emptied itself right in front of me. I leaned down to help Amanda collect her things when I saw the note we'd left her last night tucked among her things. She'd gone out of her way to make sure that I saw it. I decided to ignore it, just to see how she'd handle it.

After everything was gathered up and restored to her purse, including the note Moose and I had left her the night before, Amanda looked extremely agitated when I failed to react to it.

"Is something wrong?" I asked.

"No, everything's fine," she snapped out.

"Well, thanks again for coming by," I said with another bright smile.

Amanda was two steps from the door when she stopped, turned, and looked me dead in the eyes. "Victoria, did you come by my house last night and leave me a note?"

"A note? Why would I do that?" I asked with as much innocence as I could muster. "What are you talking about?"

She reached into her bag and deftly extracted the note Moose had written. "I'm talking about this."

"I didn't write that," I said as she tried to hand it to me. It was true, too. After all, Moose had penned it, not me.

She looked a little deflated by my denial. "Blast it all, I was sure that it was you."

"What does it mean?" I asked, stretching even my breaking point when it came to protesting my innocence.

"Who knows? Some madman is on the loose killing my ex-boyfriends. How should I know what it means?"

"Have you had more than one die lately?" I asked.

"I don't like to talk about it," she said as she stuffed the note back in her purse and closed it.

What was this all about? Had another of Amanda's boyfriends been dispatched prematurely? That might bear looking into. "I'm a good listener, or so I've been told," I said.

Amanda bit her lower lip, and after a moment's pause, she said, "I don't know what it would hurt to tell you at this point. Somebody has up and killed the last two men I've dated. The first, Kyle Keveler, was hit by a drunk driver, and you know what happened to Benny. I'm afraid that I'm cursed, Victoria. They caught the woman who killed Kyle, but if they don't catch whoever murdered Benny, and soon, I'm going to lose my mind. If there's anything I can do to help you investigate, just let me know. I want that murderer caught more badly than you do; I can guarantee you that."

Oddly enough, I believed her. "Amanda, I'd love to take you off our list of suspects, but you have to admit, it doesn't look good for you. You and Benny had a bad breakup, and you were thrown out of the theater the night he was murdered. *Anyone* could have picked up that award, so you have motive, means, and opportunity. Is there *anything* that you're not telling me?"

"Nothing," she said. "I don't blame you one bit for not

believing me. I didn't kill Benny, but I can't prove it."

"That's a shame," I said.

"Hang on a second," Amanda said with a frown, and then she bit her lip. "I never made it to Benny's dressing room that night. The police should be able to confirm when I got to the theater, and when I was thrown out. After that I was in the alley beside the building, but I never went to the back until Fred showed up. Do they have an exact time of death for Benny yet?"

"I don't, and if the police do, they haven't shared it with me yet," I said.

Amanda grabbed my arm. "Could you ask them for me? It would mean the world to me if I could get my name off every suspect list in town."

"All I can do is try," I said. I grabbed my cell phone and dialed the sheriff's number. After he picked up, I asked, "Did you ever get an exact time of death worked out for Benny?"

"We just did. Why do you want to know?"

I couldn't bear the thought of telling him the truth in front of Amanda. "Could you take this one on faith? I'll tell you the next time I see you. I promise."

There was a longer hesitation than I liked, but he finally said, "I don't know what it can hurt, since I just told Nate Barton at the paper, so everyone's going to know soon enough. We've narrowed it down to a fifteen-minute window between the last time Benny was seen alive and when his body was discovered." The sheriff gave me the parameters, and I compared it to what Amanda had just told me. She was in the clear, and if I hadn't already discovered it, so was Garret Wilkes.

"Amanda Lark didn't do it. She was being chased by Security backstage, and then she was being thrown out when Benny Booth was being murdered."

"Bravo. I was wondering if you were going to figure that out without any help from me. Nicely done."

"So, does your suspect list look like ours?" I asked.

"We've got Marcus, Sandra, and Fred left."

"I can't confirm or deny that," he said, but I could hear the smile in his voice nonetheless.

"Thanks," I said.

"What for? I didn't tell you anything that wasn't public knowledge," he replied.

"Thanks anyway," I said.

After I hung up, I said with a smile, "You're in the clear."

"Thank goodness," Amanda said. "How did you manage it?"

"You were being chased by Security and thrown out by Garret Wilkes around the time that Benny was murdered. That means that you're both in the clear."

Amanda frowned. "But doesn't that mean that Fred Hitchings is off the hook, too? After all, I didn't see him out back until well after I was thrown out of the theater."

"Not necessarily," I said. "He could have lost something and had to come back to get it, or he could have been staging his alibi after Benny was dead. For now, he stays solidly on our list."

"Who does?" Moose asked as he walked in.

Amanda surprised everyone, including herself, by hugging me. "I don't know how to thank you, Victoria."

"I really didn't do much of anything," I said honestly.

"That's not true, and we both know it." She surprised us all again by reaching up and kissing Moose on the cheek on her way out.

"What was that all about?" Moose asked me.

"Sit down. We have a lot to talk about."

"So, the list continues to dwindle," my grandfather said after I finished catching him up with what had happened in his absence. To his credit, Moose wasn't the least bit resentful that he'd missed out on the new developments. "At least it's getting a little more manageable now."

"True," I said, "but the three suspects we have left each had their own reasons to want to see harm come to Benny

Booth. Marcus could have killed the man out of jealousy, Sandra because of the nature of her tryst with Benny, and Fred because of his rivalry with the actor. But how do we narrow our field down to one?"

"I don't know offhand," Moose said. "You said that you have tickets for tonight's performance, didn't you?"

"Yes, I got them from Mrs. Murphy when she was eating here earlier. She was a big Benny Booth fan, who knows why, and she couldn't bring herself to watch Fred in his place."

"I'm sure that you're planning to take your husband again, but do you think that he'd mind if I accompanied you tonight? Now that Garret is off the hook, there shouldn't be any problem with me showing up."

"Mind? Greg would be thrilled. You're on, Moose. I just hope it's not a waste of time."

"Right now, it's the best we can do," he said.

"This is quite a bit different than the last time we were here together," Moose said that night as we walked into the theater lobby. "It's hard to believe all that has happened in such a short amount of time."

There were more than a few furtive glances our way, and I had to believe that they were because Moose was still a prime suspect in the murder investigation in a lot of people's minds. I knew he hadn't killed Benny, and he knew it as well, but we might have been the only two people there who believed in my grandfather's innocence.

"I wish we could get backstage again," I said.

"I agree that any respite from all of these stares would be nice," Moose said. "Does everyone think I'm guilty, or is it just my imagination?"

"No, I don't think that you're imagining anything at all," I said. My grandfather believed in direct talk, and I wasn't about to sugarcoat anything for him. "It's pretty clear that they all think you could have done it."

Moose smiled a little at my frankness. "You are my

granddaughter in more than name only, aren't you?"

"We've got a lot in common," I said. "We both appreciate candid conversation."

"We do," Moose said. He sized up the football players stationed at both sides of the stage, barring anyone who might try to mount those steps and interfere with the cast in their last minute preparations. "They're a big an ungainly lot, aren't they?"

"I doubt that anybody's going to try to get past them, so they serve their purpose, don't they? We could always try a distraction, if you think it would help."

"Maybe if I were thirty years younger," Moose said. "Hang on. I'll be right back."

Before I could stop him, he disappeared out the side door. I debated whether I should go after him or not, but in the end, I didn't want to go racing through the alley in my best dress. Where had he gone, though? A few minutes later, Moose returned to his seat, and from all outward appearances, he was no worse for the wear.

"What was that all about?"

"I wanted to try all of the exterior doors," he admitted. "Unfortunately, they were all locked up tight."

"That was good thinking," I said, "but next time, you might give me a heads up about what you're doing."

Moose looked over at me and smiled slightly. "Are you scolding me, Victoria?"

"No, I'm just reminding you that we're a team."

He nodded. "I apologize." My grandfather turned in his chair and looked around the auditorium. The seats were nearly full, and we still had three minutes before the performance was set to begin. "Mrs. Murphy secured some good seats, didn't she?"

We were two rows from the stage, and I wondered just how good our view would be. It felt as though we'd be staring up at the actors. "Actually, we're a little too close, for my taste."

"We're not here to watch the play, though," Moose

reminded me. "We are trying to find a killer."

"And you honestly think that us sitting this close will help our cause?"

He shrugged. "You never know." He tapped the program with one finger. "Just how bad is this going to be?"

"Well," I said after a moment's thought about how to put it, "based on what I saw two nights ago, even though Benny was not that great an actor, he was still head and shoulders above Fred. We're going to be in for a long night, but at least you haven't already sat through this thing once. I'm not sure how I'm going to make it."

"The things we do to solve a case," Moose said.

The lights began to fade, and I waited for the performance to begin. Maybe it would be better the second time, somehow. As it was, I was beginning to lose my taste for our community theater. Maybe one day Greg and I could afford to go to a real play on Broadway, but in the meantime, I'd have to adjust my expectations.

The curtain opened, and I watched again as Fred Hitchings was illuminated by a single spotlight. "In the course of a lifetime, a man leads many lies, I mean lives. This is one of them." His voice was shaking as he spoke, and muffing the opening line didn't help. I looked over and saw Moose grimacing.

"Buck up," I whispered.

"I'm trying," Moose said.

The play was too short to have an intermission, which was a real blessing. Given the opportunity, I was certain that over half the audience would have fled the poor performances. As it was, a few brave folks managed to sneak out anyway, and the rustling sounds behind us threatened to grow into a stampede. Sandra was off her game; whether because of the murder, or Fred's heavy-handed performance I couldn't say. The rest of the cast seemed to take their cues from the two leads, and it just got worse and worse as the evening wore on. If anything, this show was even worse than the last one had been, and if you'd asked me before I sat down, I wouldn't have said that was even possible.

Finally, the final curtain fell, and as the audience clapped mildly, I had to wonder if it was more for the end of the torture than any tribute to the actors or the director.

One actor was notable for her absence from the stage to collect applause, though.

Sandra Hall, for whatever reason, was gone.

"Where's Sandra?" I asked Moose as I poked his arm.

"What? Is she gone? She hasn't been on stage in ten minutes. I never noticed that she didn't show up for the curtain call. She's probably too embarrassed, if you ask me."

"What if she's running, Moose?" I asked. "Maybe she was waiting until her role was finished before she took off."

"We need to get backstage right now," Moose said as he stood and moved toward the steps. Peter Davis was at his post again, but he looked at ease and relaxed as folks started filing out.

"Peter," I said, "we need to get back there. You're not going to try to stop us, are you?"

"No, ma'am," Peter said with a toothy grin. "My job ended when that final curtain went down. You can go anywhere you want to, as far as I'm concerned."

"Thanks," I said as Moose and I brushed past him. I hunted everywhere for any sign of Sandra or Marcus, but they were both conspicuous by their absence.

Fred Hitchings was standing off to himself, and the man looked positively shell-shocked. "I had no idea how hard that was going to be the second time," Fred said. "Benny made it look easier than it was. I have to give him credit for that."

"You did just fine, Fred," I said, though it wasn't anywhere near the truth. "Have you seen Sandra?"

"She couldn't wait to get out of here," he said. "I thought she was going to pull Marcus's arm right out of its socket."

"How long ago did they leave?" I asked.

"Oh, it's been awhile."

"We need to call the sheriff," Moose said as he pulled me aside.

"Right." I snatched my cell phone out of my purse and grabbed my phone. "Sheriff Croft? This is Victoria. Moose and I are at the theater. Sandra and Marcus are on the run."

"I just heard," the sheriff said. "I had a man watching from the wings, and he just called me. He should have been backstage, but there's nothing I can do about that now. Don't worry, Victoria, we're on it."

"Do you think one of them is the killer?" I asked.

"Why else would they run?" the sheriff asked. "We'll take it from here. You and your grandfather did good work, but you should go home. I'll have someone give you a call once we find them."

"Okay. Thanks," I said, and then I hung up.

"What did he say?" Moose asked.

"They're hot on their trail," I said. "I guess our part is done."

My grandfather shook his head sadly. "It's kind of anticlimactic, isn't it?"

"Just because it doesn't end in a big shootout doesn't mean that it shouldn't feel good to have this whole thing resolved."

"Do we, though?" Moose asked. "We still don't know which one of them killed Benny."

"I've got a hunch the sheriff will break them down soon enough once he's caught up with them," I said. "In the meantime, there's nothing left for us to do."

"Let's go home, then, shall we?" Moose asked.

Something was nagging at the back of my mind, though, but I still couldn't put my finger on it. "Why don't you go on ahead? I think I might hang around a little."

"I'll stay with you, Victoria," he said. "I've got nothing better to do."

I patted his hand. "You don't have to babysit me. I'm sure that Martha would appreciate your company at home."

"Greg would like yours just as much," he said.

"No, he's playing poker tonight. As soon as he found out that he was off the hook tonight attending the performance with me, he rounded up a game. He won't be home until midnight."

"If I leave now, how are you going to get home?" Moose asked.

Peter, standing nearby, said, "I'll be glad to take you home whenever you're ready, Victoria."

"See? It's all taken care of. Go on. I'll be fine."

"If you're sure," Moose said.

"I'm positive," I answered.

Moose left, and just about the entire rest of the audience escaped as well. It was as though none of them could wait to get away from the place.

I found a seat up front and pondered the case. It wasn't as though I had any trouble seeing either Sandra or Marcus as killers. As personal fitness trainers, they each certainly had the upper body strength to dispatch Benny with ease. For that matter, so did Fred Hitchings, but at least he'd stayed around after the play was long over.

I noticed someone standing in the periphery, and I glanced over to see Peter rocking back and forth in place. "You're ready to go, aren't you?"

"Take your time," Peter said. "I promised to give you a ride home."

I noticed one of the extras hovering near him. She was a cute girl from the high school, and from the way she looked at Peter, and the way he glanced back at her, it told me that they were more than just friends. "You don't have to hang around here for me. I'm sure I can get another ride home."

"No, that's fine. I promised," Peter said resolutely.

"I'm more than happy to release you from it," I replied.

"It's okay, Peter. I can get a ride with someone else," the girl said. "I'd stay longer, but my folks are expecting me."

"Tell you what," I said. "Peter, go ahead and take the young lady home. You can swing by here and pick me up after you've dropped her off." I wasn't about to suggest that I accompany them. I had no desire to be a third wheel.

"Are you sure you wouldn't mind?" he asked, the hope clear in his voice.

"I'm sure. There's no need to hurry back, either. I'll be fine."

"Thanks, Victoria," he said as he quickly took the girl's hand in his and they made their way out. "I won't be long."

Once they were gone, it felt as though I was the only one left in the theater, at least in the audience. Getting up, I decided to take a little stroll backstage to see if what was bothering me might come to mind.

Harvey Springs, the janitor, was sweeping up in the hallway, and he looked startled to see me standing there. "You shouldn't sneak up on folks like that, Ma'am. You nearly gave me a heart attack."

"Sorry, Harvey," I apologized. "I just hate to see this all end." I meant the murder investigation more than the play's run, but he'd have no way of knowing that.

"It's always sad whenever one's in the books," he said. "Even this one."

He'd said the last bit nearly under his breath, but I'd still caught it. "It wasn't the best thing I've ever seen," I admitted with a smile.

He just laughed as he shrugged. "Next year there will be another one, and we'll all forget about this soon enough. Was there anything else you'd be needing, Ma'am?"

"No, as soon as my ride comes to pick me up, I'll be out of your hair," I said.

"Oh, stay as long as you'd like. Just cut the lights off on your way out. The front door locks automatically, so there's no need to worry about locking up. I'd offer you a ride myself, but I don't think you'd like being perched on the front of my handlebars, not in that fine dress you're wearing."

"You're riding home in the dark?" I asked.

"I've done it a hundred times before," he said, "and with

the good Lord willing, I've got a few more night rides still in me."

"Good night, then," I said.

Knowing Peter, it was tough to tell how long he'd be taking his young lady home. That left me with a little time on my hands, so I decided to nose around a little while I was by myself and see what I could see.

Chapter 15

One door was ajar as I walked down the hallway, so I decided to start there. It was the prop room, with rows of shelves stacked with the oddest things. On one shelf, a crystal ball sat beside a full suit of armor, while on another, an old fashioned typewriter was perched next to an astronaut's helmet. There was even a row of trophies used for various plays in the past, and as I neared it, one in particular caught my eye. If I hadn't seen so many images of its cousins so recently, I would have passed right by it without another thought.

Reaching behind a handful of bowling trophies and a silver cup, I pulled it out and looked at it. The intricate engravings were there as they were supposed to be, and the handles were the subtle but unmistakable wings of a genuine Jasper Award. Someone had covered the nameplate for the recipient with an odd kind of tape that must have come in layers, because the top layer had been removed, and recently, by the look of it. Holding the trophy up to the light, I tried to make out the name that had been written on the tape, but I couldn't do it. There had been a blackboard in the hallway where rehearsal dates and times had been posted. Would chalk help raise the letters? I hurried out with the trophy in my hand, grabbed the eraser, and flicked the chalk onto the tape. I couldn't make out much, but the last three letters showed up the best.

NGS.

Evidently Fred Hitchings had awarded himself a Jasper.

Carefully taking one edge of the remaining tape, I started to peel it up, but when I saw that the letters OTH were engraved on the plate, I stopped.

Was this Benny Booth's real Jasper? If it was, what had

he been killed with? I studied the photographs on the walls of past winners clutching their awards, and sure enough, this was the real deal.

That's when I remembered the pictures that Sheriff Croft had shown me from the crime scene. Unless I was mistaken, the murder weapon had simple handles, not the subtle wings that all of the originals sported.

That meant that if Fred stole Benny's award and replaced it with a similar looking prop, he was now my most likely candidate to be the murderer. How else would the real award end up in the prop room with Fred's name on it, and the fake in the dressing room used as a murder weapon? Plus, Fred was the only one of our suspects who had ever admitted to even *being* in the prop room. He'd claimed that he'd been locked out of the building after going through the prop room's back door. Had he mentioned that to explain any of his fingerprints that might turn up in a search of the room, or had he actually used the back door as a way of getting into Benny's dressing room from the outside without anyone realizing what he'd done?

The wrong people were running.

Sheriff Croft was wasting his time and manpower chasing after Sandra and Marcus.

Fred was the one he should be talking to.

I flipped open my phone, but I couldn't get reception from where I was standing in the hallway. Walking out onto the dim stage, I finally managed to get one bar of reception, and I started to dial the sheriff's number to tell him what I'd discovered.

I never got the chance, though.

"Put that down," Fred said from the wings as he stepped out onto the stage.

Ordinarily I would have ignored him and finished my call, but he was holding something in his hand that might just be a prop, but it looked very real to me.

It was a sword from one of the pirate plays, and he was wielding it as though he meant business.

"You couldn't let it go, could you?" Fred asked me as he took a step forward. "Throw your phone down on the stage."

I hit redial as I complied with his order, even though I wasn't sure who I'd called last on it. Whoever it was, I hoped that they'd hear what Fred was about to do to me. I didn't want to die, but going unavenged would be the worst thing I could imagine. If something did happen to me, I wanted my husband and my family to know who was responsible. The only weapon I had at my disposal was the Jasper Award, but I wasn't sure how I could use it to my best advantage.

"Would you like me to throw this down, too?" I asked.

"Don't you dare," he said in a petulant voice. "You shouldn't even be holding it."

This guy had clearly snapped. I looked around the stage wildly for something that might help me, and I noticed that there was a darkened square on the floor off to the side. What was that, a trapdoor? Maybe I could use it to my advantage, but first I had to lure Fred Hitchings over to it close enough to help me.

As my telephone clattered to the stage, Fred said, "I can't believe you came up with that in that crowded prop room. I couldn't get rid of that blasted trophy until everyone else was gone. Victoria, I was two minutes from getting away with it, and you had to keep nosing around until you found it. I thought my note would scare you off, but clearly that didn't work. When I got the clumsy one you left yourself, I panicked at first until I overheard Marcus telling Sandra about the duplicate message he got himself, so I figured you were bluffing."

"Why did you kill Benny, Fred? Was playing his role that important to you?"

"It should have been mine, but that's not why I did it. It all started out as a joke. I planned to swap Benny's Jasper with a prop, but he caught me in the act in his dressing room, and he accused me of being a hack actor, a ham with nothing to offer. You should have heard him. It made my blood boil! When the fool turned his back on me, I don't know what happened to me. Something just snapped! I had the prop in my hand, and I swung it at his head as hard as I could. I wanted to knock him out; I never meant to kill him."

"You killed him with the fake award, so you had to leave it by the body."

"It had his hair and blood on it, you see," Fred said in a calm, rational voice. "I thought about hitting him again with the real trophy, but the police are too clever with their science and all these days."

"What I don't get is why you didn't just throw the real Jasper away somewhere else," I said. "It's the only thing tying you to the murder."

"I couldn't exactly sneak it out under my coat, now could I? Besides, I couldn't stand the thought of destroying it. I was going to take it home and clean it up."

"That was pretty foolish of you, Fred," I said.

His hand tightened on the sword grip, and he took a step toward me. "Don't talk to me that way, Victoria. I won't stand for it, do you hear me?"

"Sorry. Take it easy, Fred," I said. "We can work something out here."

"I'm afraid that we can't, actually," Fred said. "It's unfortunate, but you've left me no choice. You have to go."

He took another step forward. If I let him get close enough with that blade, I was dead, and I knew it. I thought about using the Jasper in my hand to block his attack, but I didn't have that much confidence in my ability to fight off an armed man with an acting trophy. Instead, I threw it at him as hard as I could, and then I turned and started to run offstage.

I hit his shoulder, but I missed his face, which was my original target. I'd been hoping to break his nose with it. Worse yet, it wasn't even the side that held the sword. He rubbed his shoulder lightly as he hurried toward me and shouted, "Stop right there."

I felt the arc of the blade coming toward me, and I turned

to face him. Fred Hitchings might very well kill me where I stood, but he wasn't going to hit me from behind like he had Benny. I was going to make the man look into my eyes before he skewered me with that blade.

"I don't want to do this, but I really don't have any choice," Fred said as he cut the air in front of him with the sword. "Good bye, Victoria."

I braced myself for the stab, and the pain that was sure to follow, but suddenly, a light from the back burst out onto the stage in a tight spotlight. Fred was turning exactly the wrong way when the concentrated beam of light hit him and he was blinded by it, but I'd been facing the other way.

I knew if I ran, he'd have a chance of catching me.

It was time to fight back one last time.

Taking three steps toward him, I ducked, got behind him, and then I shoved him as hard as I could.

The next instant, Fred fell through the trap door as the sword itself clattered to the stage.

"Victoria, are you okay?" Peter asked me as he ran through the aisle and up onto the stage.

"I'm fine, thanks to you. That was perfect timing, by the way."

"I told you that I'd be back," he said with a grin. "I was going to try to tackle him when I saw what was going on, but I was afraid that you might get hurt if he saw that I was rushing him. I told you that I've worked the spotlight on more than one show. That was brilliant of you shoving him down the trapdoor."

"I couldn't have done it if you hadn't blinded him for me." I looked down through the opening, but I couldn't see much of anything. "Do you think he's dead?"

"Hang on a second." Peter disappeared backstage, and suddenly the lights all came to life. I peered over the edge, dreading the thought that Fred had escaped and was even now plotting to get us.

As soon as I saw him lying there, that worry vanished

instantly.

"Should we go down there and check for a pulse?"

"I've got a better idea," Peter said. He disappeared once more, and then he reappeared an instant later, holding a pitcher of water. "Sandra insists on a pitcher of water before every performance." He dumped the water down on Fred, who moaned when it hit him.

"My leg. It's broken. Get me out of here."

"Soon enough," I said as I looked down on him. "Peter, grab my phone, will you? I need to call the police."

"There's no need," Sheriff Croft said as he came through the back of the theater. "That was smart thinking calling me like that. I heard everything."

"I'm just glad that you made it," I said.

"I'm not sure why. It seems that you and Peter have everything under control here."

"We make a good team," I said. "What happened with Sandra and Marcus? They didn't kill Benny, so why did they run?"

"Your note spooked them," the sheriff explained. "They didn't want the murder pinned on them, and both of them have overactive imaginations. We caught up with them at the county line, but it was pretty clear that they didn't kill Benny. Boy, as soon as we caught up with them, Marcus started telling us that Sandra must have killed him, and she returned the favor just as fast. I've got a hunch that particular relationship is over after the things they said to each other." He touched my shoulder lightly as he added, "I'm glad you're okay."

"Are you kidding? I'm an emotional mess," I said.

"But she was brave when it counted," Peter said. "You should have seen her in action."

"I look forward to hearing all about it." Three of the sheriff's men came into the theater, and he directed them, "Fred Hitchings killed Benny Booth. Call the paramedics *after* you handcuff him." He stared down into the pit, and asked, "How are they supposed to get down there?"

"I'll show them," Peter said as he hurried off the stage to join them.

"You did good work on this one," the sheriff said after we were alone.

"Come on. I got lucky, and we both know it. If I hadn't stumbled across that trophy, I wouldn't have known a thing, and Fred would have gotten away with murder."

"I don't call that luck," the sheriff said. "You knew from one glimpse of a crime scene photo that the award used to kill Benny wasn't genuine, and that's more than I can say. I stared at the blasted thing for hours and I didn't see it."

"That's because you weren't exposed to the real trophies like I was," I said.

There was a sudden clamoring from the lobby door, and one of the deputies said, "Sheriff, there's a group of people here who insist on seeing your witness."

I could hear my family's voices growing louder by the second. "You'd better let them in, or you're going to have a riot on your hands, and you know it."

The sheriff nodded in agreement as he waved to the deputy. "Let them in."

The whole gang, all three generations, was there, and I was quickly enveloped in the heart of my family.

After I went over what had happened with them, I found myself nearly having the breath hugged out of me.

"I'm sorry I wasn't there for you," Moose said.

"There was no reason for you to be," I said. "I didn't know what I would find until I stumbled across it in the prop room."

The sheriff had faded back into the scenery as we had our little reunion.

Martha finally looked over and spotted him standing to one side. "Do you need Victoria any more tonight, Sheriff?"

"I'll need a statement in the morning, but she's free to go right now," he said.

"Then, may I suggest that we get out of here, family? I believe we should reconvene at the diner to finish our celebration," Martha said.

There were no disagreements, so we all left the theater together.

I wasn't sure that I'd ever be back, actually.

I myself had seen enough performances there to last a lifetime, and I didn't think that there was a soul in all of Jasper Fork who could blame me.

RECIPES

SALISBURY STEAK

This main course is a diner favorite, and one that's a real hit with my family as well. The taste is hard to beat, and we especially like to have this on a cold winter day when we're taking it easy and indulging in some of our favorite foods. The Salisbury steak goes great with crisp green beans (see below) and some smashed potatoes (featured on the next page) on the side. The gravy is created as the meat simmers, and some of my family think that is the best part!

Ingredients

1 (10.5 oz can) Condensed French Onion Soup, low sodium (divide into 1/3 and 2/3 portions)
1 to 1 ½ pounds ground beef (we like 85/15 and drain the fat after cooking)
½ cup dry bread crumbs (we use French's)
1 egg, whole, lightly beaten with a fork
1/8 teaspoon salt
1/4 teaspoon ground black pepper
1 to 2 Tablespoons olive oil

1 Tablespoon catsup
1/2 cup Condensed Beefy Mushroom Soup (Optional)
2 Tablespoons all purpose flour
1 Tablespoon water, tap, room temperature
1 Tablespoon Worcestershire sauce
¼ teaspoon dried mustard powder

Directions

Mix 1/4 to 1/3 cup of the condensed French Onion soup, ground beef, bread crumbs, egg, salt, and pepper together in a large mixing bowl. I find that my hands are the best tools for this job. Shape this mixture, and once it is combined into equal sized patties (4 to 8, depending on your preference), place them on a nonstick or sprayed cookie sheet, cover, and refrigerate for 30 to 60 minutes. After the patties are set, heat a large pan over medium to medium-high heat, add the olive oil, and then brown both sides of each patty, turning once. Don't crowd the pan too much, and brown these in shifts until they are all finished. Pour off the fat, and then set these aside.

In another bowl, mix together the flour and remaining soup (as well as 1/2 cup of the Beefy Mushroom soup if desired) until it has a smooth consistency. Next, add the catsup, water, Worcestershire sauce, and mustard powder. Return the browned patties to the pan and cover them with the sauce. Next, cover the pan, heating it to boiling and then simmering for 15 to 20 minutes, stirring occasionally.

These are great with green beans and the smashed potato recipe on the next page. Enjoy.

Makes 4-8 patties, depending on the size you choose.

Green Bean Tip: I like to take my green beans out of the can, pat them down with paper towels, and then cook them lightly in a medium-high pan with a little olive oil until they have a bit of crisp to them. These are heads above what you get straight from the can in my family's opinion.

MY CHEESY SMASHED POTATOES

This recipe was born after visiting a favorite diner of mine and ordering the cheesy smashed potatoes featured on the menu. The cook wouldn't give up her recipe, so I brought some home and tried to duplicate it myself. You might be tempted to skip the cream cheese, but that's what really makes the potatoes creamy.

Ingredients

1 to 1 ½ pounds new potatoes, red or gold, unpeeled and cut into chunks
1 package (8 oz) cream cheese, softened (we like Philadelphia)
1/3 to 1/2 cup sharp cheddar cheese, shredded (to taste)
Bacon, cooked and loosely chopped, one to two pieces
2 Tablespoons milk (whole, 2%, or 1% seem to work best for me)
1 Tablespoon butter
1 teaspoon Parmesan cheese, grated
1 teaspoon garlic powder
1 teaspoon cayenne pepper

Directions

Cook the potatoes, bringing the water to a boil, and then simmer 8 to 12 minutes, or until they are fully cooked. A fork should go into the potato easily. Drain the potatoes, and pat some of the moisture off them. They don't have to be dry, but the excess moisture should be gone. Mash the potatoes with a hand-masher until they are smooth, and then add the cream cheese, cheddar cheese, bacon bits, milk, cayenne pepper, garlic powder, and Parmesan cheese.

Continue to combine, at first with the masher and then with a spatula, until all of the ingredients are incorporated nicely.

Serve and enjoy!

Makes 6-8 servings, depending on the amount of potatoes used.

Made in the USA
Lexington, KY
14 January 2015